PUFFIN BOOKS

A Pack of Liars

Anne Fine was born and educated in the Midlands, and now lives in County Durham. She has written numerous highly acclaimed and prize-winning books for children and adults.

Her novel *Goggle-Eyes* won the *Guardian* Children's Fiction Award and the Carnegie Medal, and was adapted for television by the BBC; *Flour Babies* won the Carnegie Medal and the Whitbread Children's Novel Award; *Bill's New Frock* won a Smarties Award; *Madame Doubtfire* has become a major feature film by Twentieth Century Fox starring Robin Williams, and, most recently, *The Tulip Touch* was the winner of the Whitbread Children's Book of the Year Award for 1996.

# A Pack of Liars

## Anne Fine

PUFFIN BOOKS

PUFFIN BOOKS

Published by the Penguin Group
Penguin Books Ltd, 27 Wrights Lane, London W8 5TZ, England
Penguin Putnam Inc., 375 Hudson Street, New York, New York 10014, USA
Penguin Books Australia Ltd, Ringwood, Victoria, Australia
Penguin Books Canada Ltd, 10 Alcorn Avenue, Toronto, Ontario, Canada M4V 3B2
Penguin Books (NZ) Ltd, Cnr Rosedale and Airborne Roads, Albany,
Auckland, New Zealand

Penguin Books Ltd, Registered Offices: Harmondsworth, Middlesex, England

First published by Hamish Hamilton 1988
Published in Puffin Books 1990
11 13 15 17 19 20 18 16 14 12

Copyright © Anne Fine, 1988
All rights reserved

Filmset in Garamond

Made and printed in England by Clays Ltd, St Ives plc

British Library Cataloguing in Publication Data
A CIP catalogue record for this book is available from the British Library

ISBN 0–140–32954–4

For
C.A.P.P.N.F.

# ★ October ★

'Look at this.'

Oliver slid the letter across the desk and Laura picked it up. Although the spelling was correct, the handwriting was so frightful that Laura could barely read it in places.

17 Cat Alley<br>Sticklebury<br>10th October.

Dear Penpal,

I have been forced to write to you because I live in Sticklebury and your teacher needs one more penpal from our town to make enough to go round your class.

She happens to know my aunt, so my aunt forced me into writing this letter.

I am taller than average. I bite my nails until they bleed. It drives them mad. I have huge feet. I get on people's nerves because I fidget and squirm and twitch all day. I'm always tapping my feet on the bars of people's chairs. It drives them mad but I can't help it. My mother says I've always been restless and even as a baby I never wanted to be held and had to struggle all the time. I can't get to sleep at nights and lie there thinking extremely dark thoughts. I haven't any real friends my own age, but I get on with the boy next door – he's going to be three next week. I have this pebble I found, and I can't stop fingering it. It drives them mad.

And I have this problem. There's only a few of the stairs that I can tread on. I can't put my feet down on the ones which have the yellow swirly bit of the pattern. And the same goes for the assembly hall at school. I can't tread on some of the tiles, so I walk all funny whenever I'm in there. It drives them mad. And I can't take anything at all out of my school locker if I've touched the sides with my hand first – even if I just brush the edge the slightest bit, accidentally. So I get into trouble because I've never got the right things for gym or football. It drives them mad.

There are even worse things, but they are private.

How are you? I hope you are quite well.

Yours sincerely,
Simon Huggett

When she had finished reading the letter, Laura flattened it out on her desk top and stared at it a little apprehensively.

'Well?' Oliver's plastic spectacle frames slipped down to the end of his nose. He tipped his head back to peer at Laura through the lenses. 'What do you think?'

'Perhaps it's a joke.'

'Of course it's not a joke.' Oliver dashed the suggestion.

'No,' Laura admitted. 'It sounds real.'

She picked the letter off the desk and flicked it between her fingers.

'Just your luck, Oliver,' she commiserated. 'Twenty-one Sticklebury penpals, and you have to get the local nutter!'

'I beg your pardon?'

Oliver's tone was cool.

'Well,' Laura said. 'He can't be *normal*, can he? He's obviously wacko. Unhinged. A total basket case.'

Oliver was outraged.

'Wacko?' he said. 'Unhinged? A basket case? What do you mean? He might be a little bit nervy by nature. Even a trace over-active, perhaps. But he's perfectly *normal*.'

'Perfectly normal?' Laura stared at Oliver in

amazement. 'You must be mad!'

Oliver stared back.

'I can see,' he said coldly, 'that round here it's getting so you're considered a nut case if you don't share the same small habits and views as your neighbour!'

Then, inasmuch as it is possible whilst sitting in a double desk to turn one's back, Oliver did so.

Laura wasn't bothered. Although his waspish tongue had terrified her at the start, over the two terms she had been sitting next to Oliver Boot Laura had become accustomed to him. Ignoring his stern withdrawal, she turned her attention to the first letter from her own new penpal.

> 2D Cathedral Close
> Sticklebury

Dear Friend,

Would you like to write to me? I would like that. It would be nice. I hope you will.

How are you? I hope you are well.

Laura stifled a yawn.

Where do you live? Are there a lot of houses on your street? There are a lot of houses on my street. What is your house like? How many rooms do you have? Do you have lots of neighbours, like we do?

Laura shook her head in amazement. She had never read such a boring letter in her whole life.

Do you have any pets? I have no pets. Do you have a colour television? We do. Do you have a video? We do. Ours is new. Is yours new? We have four radio-cassette players in our house. How many do you have? We have a stereo system, too. Do you have a stereo system? We have a computer. Do you

Here, Laura turned towards Oliver and tapped him gently on the shoulder.

'Oliver,' she said. 'I want to say I'm very sorry that I said what I did about your new penpal. He clearly isn't barmy at all.'

Appeased, Oliver shifted round in the double seat.

'Mine is, though,' Laura added.

Behind his spectacles, Oliver raised his eyes to heaven.

'Laura,' he said. 'The whole point of having a penpal is to widen your horizons. If you go round thinking other people are barmy just because they are a little bit different from you—'

'Read this, please, Oliver,' Laura interrupted.

Oliver furrowed his brows to read the letter. He was a quick reader, even if he did still move his lips a little. He had soon read as far as Laura.

> We have a computer. Do you have a computer? What sort is it? We have some electric hedge shears. Do you have any electric hedge shears? We keep ours in the garden shed. Where do you keep yours? We have a microwave oven. Do you?
>> With very best wishes,
>>> Your penpal,
>>>> Philip

Oliver was silent – for him, a quite rare occurrence.

'Well?' Laura prompted. 'What do you think?'

'I think,' declared Oliver. 'That you should ask Mrs Coverley if you can swap penpals with someone else.'

Laura took no persuading. She raised her hand

and kept it in the air until Mrs Coverley admitted she'd noticed.

Mrs Coverley took her time admitting she'd noticed. Laura guessed she had probably been planning to get her marking up to date today. She'd probably hoped the whole class would sit quietly, reading the first batch of letters from their brand new penpals, and then replying to them. She'd talked quite a lot about what a good idea penpals for everybody would be. It would improve their writing, she said. It would widen their horizons. But Laura wasn't the only one in the class who suspected that she also wanted more time to mark books.

So Laura stubbornly kept her hand in the air and she could see that, out of the corner of her eye, Mrs Coverley was watching it waving about like a lonely bullrush in a rather stiff breeze.

Then Mrs Coverley lifted her own arms to tuck a stray strand of her thick pepper-and-salt hair back in her bun. And as she did so she pretended to notice Laura's hand for the first time.

'Problem, dear?'

'Please, Mrs Coverley, may I swap penpals with somebody else?'

Instantly, Mrs Coverley foresaw utter chaos. Her poor heart sank. In front of her, a dozen or more hands were immediately lifted.

'And me, Mrs Coverley!'

'Me too, please!'

'I'll swap with Laura! I'll swap with *anybody*!'

'I asked *first*!'

Mrs Coverley glanced at her watch. She had done exactly six minutes' quiet, uninterrupted marking.

She had corrected exactly three books. That meant there were exactly thirty-nine books left to correct.

On the other hand, Laura Irwin was not generally an awkward child. In fact, she was what Mrs Coverley called 'a sensitive plant'. That was the reason she had been put next to over-confident Oliver Boot. Mrs Coverley was rather hoping the two of them would rub off on one another.

'Laura,' Mrs Coverley asked. 'Why exactly do you want to change penpals with somebody else?'

Laura wondered quite how to put it. After all, Mrs Coverley had probably gone to some trouble to find them these penpals. Stumped, she nudged Oliver, who had become her guide to courteous and correct classroom behaviour.

'Tell her you very much fear that the two of you will be temperamentally unsuited to one another,' whispered Oliver.

'What was that, Oliver Boot?' asked Mrs Coverley.

But Oliver had been brought up to be fearless. Where anyone else would hastily bow their head and mutter: 'Nothing, Mrs Coverley,' Oliver repeated, unabashed:

'Laura believes that she and her new penpal might be temperamentally unsuited to one another.'

'Sometimes I think I might be temperamentally unsuited to you, Oliver Boot,' said Mrs Coverley. 'But I don't go around asking to swap classes.'

Then, simply in order to avoid having to face Oliver's reproachful look, she turned to the rest.

'Is anyone here willing to swap penpals with Laura? No, you may *not* read her letter through first before you decide. No, you may *not* change your mind immediately after. Yes, you *may* just have one swift and simple, *silent* swap.'

Almost everyone in the class raised a hand. The one lonely bullrush had turned into a clump of waving reeds.

Mrs Coverley sighed. Then, ostentatiously, she shut her eyes and lifted her felt pen in the air. She turned it over and steered it downwards in a nose-dive on the register. She opened her eyes and read aloud the name she'd stabbed with red ink.

'Zafira.'

'Goody!'

The others, disappointed, grumbled quietly amongst themselves whilst Zafira exchanged her letter with Laura's. Then everyone settled down again, and Mrs Coverley went back to her marking.

Laura untucked the flap of her new, rainbow-coloured envelope. It was with real optimism that she drew out the sheet of matching rainbow note-paper and read:

> 2A Cathedral Close
> Sticklebury
>
> Dear New Penpal,
>   I am glad to write to you. I know we shall have such fun telling one another everything exciting about ourselves. Please write back to me as soon as you can and tell me all about yourself.

On Laura's face appeared the same glazed look that had come over her when she read Philip's letter.

> I live in Sticklebury, which is very exciting because we have one of the oldest cathedrals in the country! Isn't that wonderful?

9

Laura's glazed look gave way to one of mingled scorn and disbelief.

> My house has four pink windows and one pink door. I think pink is a very nice colour, don't you?

No, Laura thought privately. As it happens, I don't. But she pressed on bravely to the end of the letter.

> What is your own house like? Please tell me when you answer my letter. How many rooms are there? Can you describe them to me, and what is in them? For example, do you have a colour television? Or a computer? Or a microwave oven? Or a stereo?

Laura stopped reading.

'Oliver?'

Oliver shook his head firmly.

'I'm busy writing to Simon,' he told her.

'Who?'

Laura was mystified.

'Simon Huggett.' Seeing her look, which was still blank, he fleshed the name out for her a little: 'You know. My new penpal. The Sticklebury nutter. The wacko. The total basket case.'

'Oh, *him*,' said Laura. 'Never mind *him*. This one is *worse*.'

So Oliver laid down his pen and picked up the letter from Laura's second penpal. And, unlike her, he read it to the bitter end:

> Have you a tape-recorder? Or a food processor? Or a chest freezer? I would be interested to know all about you and your home. I very much look forward to getting a letter from you.
>> Your friend,
>> Miranda

Once again, Oliver was momentarily silenced. Then he rallied.

'It must be something in the Sticklebury water,' he said.

'Like fluoride?'

'Worse,' Oliver said darkly. 'Far, far worse.'

Laura leaned forward in her seat, and prodded Nikhil.

'Nikhil,' she said. 'May I have a quick peep at your penpal's letter?'

'I'm busy answering it,' replied Nikhil.

'You don't need the letter sitting in front of you to write back,' pointed out Laura.

'You do with this one,' Nikhil groused. 'It's nothing but a pile of stupid, boring questions.'

Nevertheless, he passed the sheet of notepaper back over his shoulder, leaving his hand there with the fingers dangling, to hint at his hopes for its speedy return.

Oliver and Laura read this one together.

The Hermitage
Sticklebury

Dear Whoever You Are,
  What a good idea this is! I am so keen to know everything about you. You must tell me what your house is like. For example, what is your living room like? Do you have a television in it? Or a video? Or

At this point, Oliver totally lost interest. Picking up his pen, he turned back to his letter to Simon Huggett. Laura skip-read the rest of the letter and then used it to brush Nikhil's waiting fingers, which closed around it like the tentacles of a sea-anemone sensing the presence of plankton.

Nikhil grunted his thanks. Laura picked up her pen and sighed. So *this* was what having a penpal meant. The sheer, grisly tedium of posting drivel like this to one another for months on end, possibly for *years*. She simply couldn't bear it. Why couldn't she have ended up with someone interesting, like Simon Huggett? Why did she have to get this dreary Miranda?

Laura picked up her pen.

> 21 Acacia Avenue
> Westburn

Dear Miranda,
    Thank you for your nice letter. Now I will tell you all about myself. My name is La—

Oh, it was hopeless! She simply couldn't churn the stuff out. She had cramp in her hand already. There *must* be some escape.

Suddenly, a little thought struck Laura. She hesitated for a moment. A smile spread over her face. She hesitated a moment longer – and she was lost.

> – dy Melody Estelle Priscilla
Hermione Irwin, but you must only write L. (short for Lady) Irwin on your envelopes or I shall be embarrassed, since I do not use my title in class. It irritates the teachers so, to have to keep calling one 'Lady Melody' the whole time.
    I live in a small palace

Here, Laura stopped and sucked her pen, and thought. Best not to go right over the top straight away, she decided. Best not to live in a palace, however small.

She took a spare ink cartridge from her pencil box, held it above the word *palace* and squeezed out a small blot of ink. It fell exactly on the second letter.

> I live in a small place in the town. (I do apologise for that unsightly ink blot; the little lad who sits beside me will keep jogging my elbow.) It only has three floors, but Mother says that what with the servant problem as it is today, it's probably just as well that the house is so compact. And anyway, as soon as term ends we always go to stay with Grandmother in her huge country mansion.

Laura was writing steadily now – no sign of cramp.

> Sadly, since poor Father's sudden and shocking disappearance, we have been penniless. This is the reason why I now attend this rather dismal and unpleasant school, instead of the great and expensive boarding academy in the country where I was allowed to keep both my ponies. But we still do have a lot of nice things left over from the good old days.

Here, Laura stopped and read Miranda's letter through again before carrying on:

> No, we do not have a television set. Or a video. My mother believes that they are filled with noxious rays that are very bad for the body, and equally noxious programmes that are equally bad for the soul. We do not have a stereo. Or a cassette record player. Or a microwave. Or any of the things you mention. We do not, however, have a totally empty house. We have some perfectly lovely old French furniture, and a lot of charming china and delicate glassware. Grandmother still has her diamonds, and Mother her priceless furs. But my father's collection of

ivory snuff boxes has been taken off the marble mantelpiece under the stuffed tigers' heads on the wall, and been put away under the stairs where the sight of it can no longer upset my sorrowing mother. My own set of Chinese porcelain dolls has to be kept under my four poster bed with the velvet drapes, because the rest of the house is so bursting with fancy knick-knacks and precious possessions that there is scarcely room to turn around.

Laura looked at the clock. Eleven forty-five! How time could fly!

We do have a pet, yes. An Irish wolfhound, and her name is—

Laura turned to Oliver.

'How do you spell those old rulers of Russia before the revolution?'

'C-z-a-r-s,' came the automatic response. 'Or C-z-a-r-i-n-a-s.'

Since Oliver failed to look up from his own writing to deliver this information, he failed to catch Laura's grateful nod.

Laura loved sitting next to Oliver. She'd had a difficult time in school until Mrs Coverley decided to put her beside him. She had been painfully shy. She'd hated answering questions wrongly, or making any sort of mistake; and not knowing whether or not she ought to raise her hand with a query was a torment. But since she'd shared a desk with Oliver Boot, her life had changed. He knew the answer to almost every question she ever asked him, and, on the very rare occasions when he didn't, she knew for certain it must be a reasonable problem with which to bother Mrs Coverley. She'd been a happier child since she was, as she still tenderly thought of it, 'given Oliver'. She wouldn't offer to swap desks with anyone, now.

> We do have a pet, yes. An Irish wolfhound, and her name is Czarina. With me, she is as gentle as a kitten. With strangers, however, she is fierceness incar—

'Oliver,' said Laura. 'How do you spell incarnate?'

Oliver's fist slid to a halt in the middle of the word that he happened to be writing.

He pushed his spectacles back up the slope of his nose, and looked at Laura curiously.

'*Czars?*' he said, '*Czarinas? Incarnate?* What are you writing to this penpal?'

'I'm telling her about my Irish wolfhound, Czarina, who is fierceness incarnate.'

Oliver narrowed his eyes and stretched out a hand. He laid it against Laura's forehead, which was quite cool.

'Laura,' said Oliver. 'You don't have an Irish wolfhound called Czarina who is fierceness incarnate. You have a rather mangy old tomcat called Mr Whiskers who is generally asleep.'

'Just a moment, Oliver,' murmured Laura politely. 'I've almost finished. I'll be with you in a minute.'

She was hastily scribbling down her last few sentences.

> fierceness incarnate. After my father's sudden and shocking disappearance, to which I have already referred, Czarina has become the guardian of our family.
> I have no brothers and sisters, and

therefore I am somewhat lonely. And so, Miranda, you will easily understand what a true pleasure it is for me to have a brand new penpal like yourself.

Yours most affectionately,
Lady Melody
(or L. Irwin)

Laura considered sketching a small but distinguished coat of arms underneath Lady Melody's frilly signature, but decided against the idea on the grounds that it was vulgar. She laid down her pen and glanced hopefully at Oliver, but he was still writing.

To pass the time, she read Simon Huggett's letter through a second time, shuddering gently at the thought of him. Oh, all that fidgeting and twitching and chewing the bleeding fingernails! All that insomnia and pebble-fingering and not being able to step on the yellow swirls in the carpet, or take his football gear out of his locker. And even worse things that were private. He'd be enough to drive anyone mad, Laura reckoned, and wondered what on earth Oliver had found to say to him, except, *For God's sake, pull your socks up.*

But Oliver was already on his third page!

Surreptitiously, Laura knocked the two finished sheets of Oliver's reply with her elbow, swivelling them round on the desk until they lay at an angle at which she could read what he had written.

8 Green Lane
Westburn

Dear Simon Huggett,

All of the little habits you describe in your letter are perfectly normal. What is not quite so normal is telling perfect strangers about them.

16

Good old Oliver Boot, thought Laura. Straight out to bat.

> If you fidget and squirm and twitch all day while kicking the furniture and chewing your nails down to the quick, you are bound to irritate adult people, who are extremely sensitive, and especially your parents, who may feel guilty and responsible, and worry that you have become the way you are because of the way they treated you as a baby, or brought you up.

Or think you are just wacko, Laura thought privately.

> In spite of what all the books say, you might *never* grow out of all these horrible habits. *Ever*. You only have to look about you on a bus to see grown-ups with bitten fingernails fidgeting and twitching horribly. The thing is, when you are grown up, other people dare not be so rude as to let on that they are being driven mad. They simply get up and change seats. *Your* problem is that none of the people who are being driven mad by you can escape. The others in your class can't just get up and walk out when they have had enough of your squirming and banging. Neither, unfortunately for them, can your parents.

Poor Simon Huggett, Laura thought, getting this stone-cold comfort through his letter box.

> There is nothing at all unusual in not being able to bring yourself to tread on certain floor tiles or yellow swirly bits in the carpet, or having to take things out of your locker in exactly one particular way. What *is* unusual is telling other people. It is much more normal to leave them to notice for themselves. For example, I myself have

noticed that Laura, who sits beside me in class and is a sensitive plant by nature, has to run her fingers lightly along every single bar in the school railings when we go home at the end of the day. If she misses one out, I have to stand and wait and pretend I haven't noticed while she makes some feeble excuse to go back to the door and start again.

That's nice, thought Laura. Tell the *world*.

If you can't sleep at night, you're probably being sent to bed too early because they can't stand any more of the sight of you twitching and chewing. Everyone lies in bed thinking. It is perfectly normal. So are extremely dark thoughts. It is extremely dark, after all. It is also not at all unusual to get on well with two-year-olds next door, if you have any; though, once again, it is not quite so normal to admit it.

Laura leaned closer to Oliver in order to read the last paragraph, as he wrote it, over his shoulder.

You cannot be held in the slightest responsible for your height or the abnormal size of your feet.
    Yours very sincerely,
      Oliver Boot.

'Is that *it*?' Laura asked, incredulous.

Oliver, she could tell at once, was more than a little put out by her response.

'What do you mean: "Is that *it*?" What's wrong with it?'

'What's wrong with it? Only that there's poor old Simon Huggett getting in terrible trouble for picking his way across the dining hall like a paralysed crab, and playing football in his socks, and even worse things that are private. And all you have to say is: "It's perfectly normal"!'

'He's quite miserable enough as it is,' Oliver pointed out tartly. 'He doesn't need his new penpal to make him feel worse.'

But Laura was by no means satisfied.

'But he needs help. He wants *advice*.' She tapped the letter with her fingertips. 'He's practically poured his heart out in here!'

Oliver was getting a little bit hot under the collar.

'How can I advise him? I've never even met him. For all I know, he could be a cat strangler, or sleep in a coffin, or think he's a werewolf. What *are* these even worse things that are private?'

Laura was really excited now.

'Ask him! Poor Simon's clearly dying to tell, and get them off his chest. So *ask* him!'

Oliver was dubious.

'I'm not sure, really. . . .'

'For heaven's sake, Oliver! If you won't, I will!'

And in a most unusual act of boldness, Laura whipped away the last page of Oliver's letter and flattened it on her part of the desk. Oliver made no move to stop her, even when she reached out for his pen and unscrewed the top. Or when she wrote, under his signature:

P.S.

She hesitated, looking at Oliver as though for permission.

Oliver just shrugged.

So Laura wrote, in neat capital letters that could just as well have been Oliver's, one final sentence:

19

Then she folded up all three sheets of the letter
and slid them into the envelope. Before Oliver
could change his mind and stop her, she sealed the
flap.

'There!' she said. 'Now we'll find out.'

Oliver picked up Laura's own letter to Miranda.

'If you can add postscripts to mine, I can read
yours,' he bargained.

'Go ahead,' Laura offered. She was quite proud
of her Lady Melody letter, and happy for Oliver to
read it. She twisted in the seat to watch his face.

It was a picture. Early confusion soon gave way
to utter bafflement, and then astonishment and
shock. His lips moved slightly as he read the words.
His eyebrows knitted, and he frowned. But Laura's
cheerful anticipation of his amusement and com-
mendation turned to disquiet as she watched his
frown steadily deepen, and his face grow dark. By
the time his eyes had reached the bottom of the
page, she felt thoroughly nervous. What was the
matter? What on earth had she done?

'You've told a pack of lies!'

His shock was evident. He was scandalised.

'It's just one terrible lie after another. It's nothing
to do with the truth. What have you done?'

Now it was Laura's turn to be put out.

'Don't be so silly, Oliver. It's only a joke.'

Oliver's face cleared.

'So you're not sending it?'

'Of course I'm sending it! Why should I write
two whole pages for nothing?'

'But none of it's true.'

Laura was exasperated.

'Of course it's not true. I never said it was. But at least it's not boring.'

'But it's just lies.'

Laura flushed hotly.

'It isn't lies,' she insisted. 'Not really *lies*. You're simply fussing. What does it matter what I write to a penpal I've never met and never will meet?'

'You can't write lies,' repeated Oliver. 'You can't just write *a pack of lies*!'

In his excitement, he allowed his voice to shoot up above the murmuring undertones that Mrs Coverley always pretended not to hear. She raised her head.

'Trouble?' she asked them both sweetly.

'No,' Laura and Oliver answered promptly. 'Thank you, Mrs Coverley.'

'Good. Back to your letters, dears.'

And Mrs Coverley returned to her marking.

Oliver hissed in Laura's ear:

'I'm telling you, you'd better not hand in that letter to be posted!'

To his astonishment, Laura snapped back:

'Don't tell me what to do, Oliver Boot!'

The sharp tone carried. Keeping her head tucked well down over the exercise books she was marking, Mrs Coverley permitted herself a small, secret smile.

But Laura spoke with a good deal more confidence than she felt. It didn't come easily to her to ignore any of Oliver's usually sound advice. And when, a few moments later, Mrs Coverley closed the last book with relief, and strolled around the classroom collecting their replies to their penpals,

Laura found herself making an excuse not to give in her letter.

'I haven't quite finished. May I post it at home?'

'You won't forget, dear?'

'No, I'll remember.'

So Mrs Coverley moved on.

And it turned out that Laura was by no means the only person not to have finished her letter. When Mrs Coverley returned to her desk, she had only six sealed envelopes but an earful of excuses.

'You are a nuisance,' she scolded them as the bell rang. 'Last term you all claimed you were very keen on this idea. I went to a great deal of trouble following up an advertisement I saw for twenty penpals. I even had to find one extra. And all I've heard as I walked round this classroom is how boring and stupid they are. You're all very ungrateful.'

At any other time of the day, she might have harangued them all for a little longer; but since she wanted to get home, she didn't bother to dwell on the point.

Even before Laura had reached the cloakroom, Oliver was attacking her.

'Lying is wrong.'

'Not always,' Laura tried to defend herself.

'Yes, it is. Give me one single example of when a lie would not be wrong.'

He stood, deliberately blocking the cloakroom doors, his face plastered with the complacent smirk of someone sure he's completely in the right. Laura couldn't help thinking what a smarty-boots he looked; and, as she pushed past him, she also couldn't help thinking of an example.

'Suppose a man frothing at the mouth and carrying a blood-stained hatchet forced his way into the playground and wanted to know which way Mrs Coverley had gone. You wouldn't tell him she'd just gone in the staff lavatories, would you? You'd say she'd gone home with a terrible headache.'

Oliver was looking a bit less smug by the time she she had finished. But he did try to argue.

'That's a bit rare, isn't it? A bit unlikely? You can't judge by that. It wouldn't happen hardly *ever*.'

It wasn't really Laura's fault that another example immediately sprang to mind.

'Suppose you were a famous jungle explorer who got separated from your mate, and went thrashing through the undergrowth for days, completely lost, until a tribe of natives found you. Suppose they were a bit nasty-tempered, but they invited you to share their meal. Then it turned out they were cannibals, and what was on the menu was your mate's leftover fingers and thumbs dipped in mashed bananas and fried in the pot. Couldn't you tell a tiny white lie, and say that eating fried bananas was against your religion?'

Oliver was getting red-faced now. But Laura, unwisely, had got into her stride.

'Suppose a farmer had to keep absolutely still for a really important injection after a nasty tractor accident. And just as they slid the needle into his arm, he asked if his precious sheepdog Flossy was safe and sound. You'd say she was, wouldn't you? Until the needle was out? Even if you weren't quite sure?'

'Shut up,' said Oliver. 'Just shut up, Laura.'

'Suppose,' persisted Laura. 'That you were ship-wrecked on a desert island with a kind-looking old lady who had a million pounds in cash in her handbag. And since neither of you thought that you would ever be rescued, so no one would ever know, this kind-looking old lady told you one night beside the campfire that she was actually the secret leader of a fiendish terrorist organisation, and she'd planned to use all that money in her handbag to make bombs. And then one day the old lady was bitten by a snake and died a horrible, lingering death. But the very next day you and the money were rescued by passing sailors. And when you got back to the city, all of the old lady's lawyers and relations asked what she had wanted to do with the money, so they could act on her wishes. You'd say she told you she was going to build a lovely new swimming pool for the local orphanage, wouldn't you?'

But Oliver was striding out of the cloakroom in a terrible temper, banging the door behind him.

'Some people,' Laura called after him, 'just can't handle a perfectly reasonable discussion.'

The moment the words popped out, Laura regretted them. It was one thing to argue Oliver down, but quite another to rub it in. And anyway, in her heart of hearts Laura knew perfectly well that Oliver was right. In spite of all her ridiculous examples, it was wrong to lie. And that was obvious. Because you never had to make up fancy, far-fetched examples to prove it was sometimes all right to tell the truth, did you? And if someone bellowed across the playground that you were a truthful person, you wouldn't mind at all. But if you thought people were even whispering that you were a liar, you'd *hate* it.

Laura pushed open the cloakroom door, and, blinking against a shaft of bright October sunlight, made her way up the steps into the playground. Hardly anyone was about. It was pretty chilly, and most of the class had rushed off home to warmth and television and tea. Only Nikhil and Kevin were still hanging about, stamping on old juice cartons in the gutter. They were waiting for Kevin's twin sister Chrissie, who was crouched by the gates, rethreading half of a snapped shoelace.

But they all lived in the other direction. Usually Laura walked home with Oliver, but he was nowhere to be seen. She was so upset that he seemed to have taken the quarrel seriously enough to set off without her that she clean forgot to brush her fingertips against the first few bars of the railings as she went past.

When she realised, she was torn. She hadn't known that Oliver had noticed this little habit of hers, and it embarrassed her to have to retrace her steps and start again. She even found herself glancing at her fingertips, as though to check she had not become like the dreaded Simon Huggett in yet another way and turned into a terrible nailbiter.

But when at last she reached the gates again, she found Oliver sitting cross-legged on the other side, patiently waiting. Laura expected at least a bit of needling about the delay; but Oliver made it perfectly clear that the last thing he wanted was to resume hostilities. He said nothing at all, and just fell quietly in step with her along the pavement under the crisp and yellowing trees.

Laura, for her part, smiled apologetically.

They walked in silence for some time, kicking leaves. Then Oliver offered:

'Pity about your Lady Melody letter, though. It was very colourful. I particularly liked all that stuff about jewels and priceless furs and ivory snuff boxes and porcelain dolls.'

'Good, wasn't it?' agreed Laura. She sighed. 'It seems a terrible waste not to send it. . . .'

Part of her still hoped that Oliver would change his mind, and start encouraging her to post it.

'Terrible,' Oliver sympathised. He reached out to snap a bunch of scarlet berries off a bush, and popped them, one by one, between his fingers, making them spurt. 'But think how Miranda would feel if she found out. She'd think you'd treated her very badly.'

'I don't think she'd mind,' Laura argued. 'It's only a joke.'

'The reason you think she wouldn't mind is because it's *her* that's being fooled, and not you,' Oliver scoffed. 'You'd look at it differently the other way round. If you really want to know whether Miranda would mind or not, then you should ask yourself how *you* would feel if she did the same to you.'

'I wouldn't mind.'

'Really?'

Laura picked at a brilliant red leaf. It crackled between her fingers as she shredded it to the spine. Would she mind? If she received a letter like the one she had written today, she knew she'd spend a good deal of her time thinking and wondering about the person who wrote it. *And* she'd write back at once. She'd make a real effort, too, to write a proper reply – something open and sympathetic that didn't just ignore the sad and lonely bits like the sudden and shocking disappearance of a father, or the loss of two ponies – but something that wasn't too gloomy, either. A reply that was both understanding and cheerful. It would probably take ages. And she'd be bound to make a few silly and tactless mistakes the first time around, and have to copy the whole thing out all over again. It would probably take forever.

So what if, after all that trouble and effort, she found out the letter was just a joke?

Well, she wouldn't think it was funny, that was for sure. In fact, she'd be livid. She'd feel deeply offended and very, very angry indeed. She'd find it very hard to forgive anyone who made such an idiot of her.

'I'd *hate* it.'

'I thought so.'

Oliver relapsed into a cheerful kicking of dead leaves, and it was Laura herself who, after a moment's thought, picked up the topic again.

'I don't like jokes like that.'

'I know you don't. Do you remember when Chrissie told you that Mr Whiskers had been squashed by a car?'

'I sat down in the playground and burst into tears!'

'And then she grinned and waggled her hands and said: "Fooled you!".'

'And I got up and punched her on the nose!'

'Really *hard*.'

'I wouldn't have minded if it had been April

27

Fools' Day. You *expect* to be told lies then.'

'Like when you go to a market or a bazaar, and all the stall keepers swear on the graves of their grannies the goods are solid gold, and half price!'

'You don't mind. You expect it. It's *understood*. It's quite different from being told lies by someone you ought to be able to trust.'

Laura's memory of her humiliation in the playground was far too vivid to be ignored. She rooted in her schoolbag, and drew out the Lady Melody letter.

'I'm going to throw it away,' she told Oliver firmly.

They looked round for a litter bin. But there were none. And Laura never dared throw anything down in the street when Oliver was watching. He always picked it up again, making her feel terrible. So she carried the offending letter as they walked on.

At the corner they separated, and Laura went on alone. Still there was no litter bin in sight. Yet every few yards along the street there was some sort of post. You wouldn't reckon, Laura thought, it would be too much trouble or cost the earth to hang a litter bin on one of them. What were they all, anyway? She looked at the posts with fresh interest. A few, of course, were just plain, slim, concrete lampposts. Others were parking signs. That was a bus stop. This one was definitely home made, with a board nailed to it that said *House For Sale*. That one was a lamp-post, too; but there was a sign fixed firmly to the pole:

## TAKE CARE
## THIS IS A
## NEIGHBOURHOOD WATCH
## STREET

What was a Neighbourhood Watch Street, for heaven's sake, she wondered, before remembering all the talk at home, and all the fuss in the local paper, about spates of robberies across the town. It seemed that every now and again there'd be a rash of burglaries – sometimes as many as ten houses in the same street. And then the neighbours panicked and held a meeting at which they agreed to keep their eyes open for people acting suspiciously or strangely. And they hoped to warn off the burglars with these signs.

Laura wondered if this meant that she herself were being watched from over hedges or behind curtains. Creepy idea! If Oliver saw a net curtain twitch as he walked by, he'd glower menacingly over the wall. But Laura hadn't been brought up fearless, like Oliver. And with her quest for a litter bin entirely forgotten, she found herself walking faster and faster until she turned safely into her own street and saw Mr Whiskers curled, wrapped in slumber, on top of next door's garden wall.

Stuffing the Lady Melody letter back in her schoolbag, she scooped him up. He didn't wake. He rarely did. Oliver scathingly referred to him as 'Comatose Cat', but Laura was secretly grateful that Mr Whiskers stayed cradled in her arms, warm and so comforting, just like a great, fat, rumbling muff, while she fished the doorkey out of her pocket and, waving to Mrs Bandaraina next door, let herself into the cold and uninviting house. She hated coming home to no one – no lights, no music playing softly in the kitchen. But sometimes her mother had to work late, and her father was never home before six. It made a difference having Mr Whiskers, even if he was fast asleep.

Laura carried him with her round the downstairs rooms, switching on lights. She kept on cuddling him while she made toast, even though it was awkward. He stirred from torpor, briefly, to lick the butter from her fingertips. To keep him happy in her arms, she let him. And only when the house seemed warmer and somehow more friendly did she tip him onto the floor, and fill his milk dish and his feeding bowl.

While Mr Whiskers ate, Laura glanced at the clock. Even though she and Oliver had dawdled practically all the way home, there was over an hour to wait before she could expect her father. Her mother always said that if Laura felt the slightest bit nervous or lonely she was to go round to Oliver's house, and stay there until her father turned up to collect her. But Oliver's family made Laura feel even more jittery than being on her own in an empty house. All of them were always so busy being fearless. It was hair-raising to hear Oliver's mother ranting at her local councillor down the phone, or watching Oliver's father writing his bitter letters to the newspapers. Even Oliver's baby sister, who was just learning to walk, seemed to have nerves of steel. So Laura preferred the other arrangement, whereby she was allowed to come home as long as Mrs Bandaraina next door kept an eye on her over the fence. That way, at least, there was plenty of time to get homework done.

And to write letters. . . .

Oh, dear. Laura sighed. Best get it over with.

She pulled Miranda's achingly dull letter out of her schoolbag.

> Have you a tape recorder? Or a food processor? Or a chest freezer? I would be interested to know all about you and your home.

How to begin?

The trouble was, Laura decided, gazing around the kitchen and through the door into the sitting room, that, unlike Lady Melody's small place in town, her own home was, like Miranda's letter, quite without interest. There was simply nothing to tell a penpal.

Who could possibly care to know about anything in here, thought Laura, staring around in quiet desperation, and ticking the boring inventory off on her fingers.

> One boring sink
> Two boring taps
> One boring fridge
> Acres of really boring wallpaper
> A boring window with a boring tree outside
> A boring floor with a matching boring ceiling
> A boring oven and a boring radiator

Etcetera, etcetera, etcetera, all totally boring.

But she *must* write a letter. What was it Mrs Coverley always said when people lifted their hands and complained that they couldn't think of anything to write? 'Then *don't* think. Just get that old pen moving.'

Right, Laura told herself firmly. Right! Off we go.

21 Acacia Avenue
Westburn

Dear Miranda,
   My name is Laura Irwin and I am an only
child.

The old pen stopped moving. That was about
all Laura could think of to say.
   She read Miranda's letter through again for inspiration. It wasn't at all inspiring – still less on second
reading than on first. But she could at least do
what Nikhil had done, and answer all the boring
questions.

> I live in a boring house on a boring street. It
> has six boring rooms, not counting the
> boring bathroom, and all of them are pretty
> boring.

This sounded so rude that Laura ripped it up
and started her reply all over again.

21 Acacia Avenue
Westburn

Dear Miranda,
   My name is Laura Irwin, and I am an only
child. I used to wish I had an elder brother,
but now I've stopped because I've seen the
way they can treat you.
   I live with my mum and dad in a plain
house on a plain street.
   My father drives around all day for Forrest
Trade Deliveries. Sometimes he takes me
with him at weekends.

He might even take her with him this weekend.
She loved these trips. Sometimes they stopped off
at garden centres to pick up plants and equipment
for Mum.

> My mum's a gardener. She's not so busy at
> this time of year because the spring and
> summer panics are over, and most things will
> soon be neatly shrivelling up for the winter.

Including me, thought Laura. It isn't very warm
in here. Why isn't the heating working properly?

> My mum and dad put central heating in last
> year, but we don't have most of the other
> things you mention. Except for the telly, of
> course. And the stereo. We did have a tape
> recorder, but my mum took it to be fixed, and
> forgot it. They've lost it now.

How boring can a letter get? Never mind. No
need to feel guilty. However bad it was, it was
better than Miranda's letter to her. And, though
short, it would have to do.

> I have to go now. Please write back soon.

Please don't. Please, please, *please* don't.

> Love,
> Laura Irwin.

There. Duty done.

With the most massive sigh of relief, Laura
addressed the envelope, and searched for a stamp.
There were none in the cabinet drawer. There
might be some upstairs in her parents' bedroom,
but it would have to wait. She wasn't going up
there. All of the windows gleamed so blackly. The
house seemed horribly empty and quiet. She'd stay
downstairs and turn the telly on, and she and Mr
Whiskers would sit and watch, whatever it was.
*Surely* her father would come home soon. Surely
the fifth pair of car head-lights that chased through
the window and across the living room wall would
be his – well, maybe the tenth pair.

His was the eighth car to come down the street. She knew it was him because the lights brushed over the wall in quite a different direction as he swung the car round into the garage. He swept in only a few moments later with an armful of provisions for supper, the enormous book of maps, and his keys. Droplets of wet from the tree by the garage glistened on his hair, and as he shook himself like a spaniel and kicked the door firmly closed behind him, he seemed to banish all the threatening blackness outside, and all of her waiting, too.

'Lucky to have me home at all, you are,' he announced, pulling his packages out of the grocery bag one by one. 'I nearly slit my throat this afternoon, stuck in a Sticklebury traffic jam.'

'You've been to Sticklebury today? There and back?'

'I almost didn't get back.' He was peeling off his jacket now, and tying on the colourful wraparound kitchen pinafore. 'I tell you, Laura. It's about time they pulled down that crumbling old pile they call Sticklebury Cathedral, and built a brand new city flyover.'

'My penpal lives in Sticklebury,' said Laura. She was trying to divert his attention as she slid her fingers across the table to steal a fresh green runner bean.

'Get off!' Her father slapped her hand. 'I haven't enough as it is.' Then he added: 'I didn't know you had a penpal.'

'I got her today. She's called Miranda, and she's deadly boring.'

'Boring?'

'On about videos and electric hedgecutters and

34

microwave ovens all the time. They all are. Oliver thinks it must be something in the Sticklebury water.'

Her father ran the cold tap over the beans.

'If they've made the same hash of their water system as they have of their roads,' he grumbled, 'I shouldn't be surprised. There must be something odd about Sticklebury folk. Anyone sensible would have got out by now, and gone to live somewhere with a nice four-lane by-pass.'

Laura nodded, barely listening. She and her mother were quite accustomed to the fact that his views on every city and town in the surrounding four counties were coloured by having to drive through them day after day.

'I had to write back,' Laura said. 'I only just finished. It would have been posted already, except—'

Suddenly she couldn't be bothered to explain all about the Lady Melody letter, and Oliver's views about lying, and the quarrel and everything. None of it mattered any more.

'Except I haven't got a stamp,' she finished lamely.

'There's some in the car.'

Laura looked out. Now rain was spattering against the window panes, and it was absolutely pitch dark out there.

Her father saw her nervous look. He held out his hand.

'Give it to me,' he told her. 'I'll stick a stamp on it in the morning, and drop it in some pillar box as I drive past.'

'Probably in Sticklebury!'

'No, thank you!' he said fervently. 'I shan't have to go back that way until November!'

Laura fished in her schoolbag and pulled out the envelope addressed to Miranda. She handed the letter to her father, who groped through the folds of the pinafore and tucked it away in his back trouser pocket.

Good riddance! Laura thought. Take your time writing back, Miranda! We might have a video by then. Or some hedgeclippers.


And that was how it came about that the wrong letter was posted. Instead of the plain account of her real house and family that Laura had fully intended to send, it was the Lady Melody letter that Mr Irwin dropped in a pillar box early the following morning.

By the time Laura realised, it was too late. It was a full three days later when she finally noticed the real letter lying undisturbed amongst the clutter on the kitchen cabinet, addressed but still unstamped.

Appalled, Laura could scarcely bring herself to touch it.

'Dad!' she called, horrified. 'Dad! What did you do with that other letter I gave you?'

Mr Irwin assured her promptly: 'No need to panic. I dropped it in a post box. Don't worry.'

No need to panic? *Don't worry*? She had just sent a pack of lies to a total stranger!

Laura spent the whole of the rest of October not daring to confess to Oliver.

# ★ November ★

I t was not until the first week in November that replies from the Sticklebury penpals began to trickle in to class.

Oliver's letter from Simon was first to arrive. It ran to four sides, and the handwriting looked, if possible, even more straggly than before.

17 Cat Alley
Sticklebury

Dear Oliver Boot,
    You shouldn't have said in your letter that I might never grow out of my horrible habits because my mother read that bit by mistake, and my father had to give her a whisky to stop her crying.
    How are you? I am very well. I have been sent to the ~~psi~~ ~~psyich~~ ~~pchi~~ ~~pci~~ psychologist because of the worse things that were private. So they aren't quite so private any more.
    I tell terrible lies. It drives them mad, but I can't help it. I also run away from school. Quite often. But then I did them both at the same time, and that was a mistake. I ran away from school after morning assembly, and my next door neighbour pounced on me while I was half in and half out of the downstairs lavatory window, sneaking back in our house. I told her the school nurse sent me home because I had head lice, which was the only thing I could think of. But that evening the next door neighbour told Mum that I mustn't come round and play with her little Peter any more till I'd been sorted out. And Mum said: Sorted Out About What? And she said: About The Headlice, Of Course. And then my mum went up the wall.
    I begged her not to, with real tears in my eyes, but she wrote to the school nurse anyway, demanding an explanation and an apology. But I just happened to lose the

letter inside a dustbin as I walked past it. I needn't have bothered, because Mum was so angry she phoned the school anyway. And when my teacher said: Simon, Where Is The Letter From Your Mother? I just panicked and told her my mother wasn't really my mother at all because I am a long lost, secret son of Prince Charles, and my mum and dad just pretend I am theirs to save the Queen and the Queen Mother from unbearable embarrassment.

So then my teacher said: Oh Yes? all sarcastically. And I panicked some more and said I could prove it with my handwriting. It is this bad because I am by nature left-handed, I said, and I am forced to write with my right hand to keep up my disguise.

All Right, my teacher said. Here Is A Pen, Simon. Write With Your Left Hand. So I asked: What Shall I Write? and she said tartly: How About This Is A Shocking Pack Of Lies?

So I wrote with my left hand, and it was even worse than this, if you can imagine. And when I said it was simply because I hadn't had enough practice writing with my left hand, my teacher went right up the wall.

So then my mum and dad came into school and saw the teacher and the nurse and the headmistress, and they all said perhaps I ought to have just a little chat with the school psi psyich pchi pci psychologist. She made me look at dots and stuff, and draw pictures of my family for her; and then she brought in my mum and dad and told them she thought I just needed a little bit more self-esteem, which is confidence.

So Mum went off and bought me a really good camera so I can get some self-esteem taking photos. And my dad got pretty ratty, I can tell you. He said that, in *his* day, if you told lies you got a really good clip round the

ear, not a really good camera. And he stopped
my telly for a whole week.

So I have spent quite a lot of time with this
new camera. Mum buys the film, but only on
condition I don't tell Dad. My photos are not
quite so awful as they were at first, and I
think my self-esteem might be getting a little
bit better.

How are you? I hope you are quite well.
    Yours sincerely,
    Simon Huggett

Laura and Oliver looked at one another over the
letter, speechless. Then Laura shrugged. Oliver
shrugged back. For once he seemed to have nothing
to say. But later in the day, Laura noticed him
drawing the letter out of his half of the desk and
reading it through again, shaking his head in
wonder and muttering to himself softly:

'They really ought to be doing something about
testing that Sticklebury water. . . .'

The next letter was from Nikhil's penpal. It came
a couple of days later. Nikhil brought it with him
to school, and glumly handed it to Oliver and
Laura, hoping for sympathy.

The three of them huddled together in a corner
of the bike shed, sheltering from the cold morning
drizzle, while Laura and Oliver read it, and Nikhil
felt sorry for himself.

The Hermitage
Sticklebury

Dear Nikhil,
    I knew this would be such a good idea! I
love getting letters. Please write again and
tell me more about your family. Do you go
out together at weekends? We sometimes go
out for the whole afternoon. And the
evenings. Sometimes we all go out together
in the evenings. Do you?

41

And tell me more about your granny who lives with you. Is she *very* old? Can she still get about? Or is she stuck at home all day in a wheelchair or in bed? Is she deaf? Or can she hear really quite well for her age? Which bedroom is she in? The one that overlooks the street? Or one of the two back ones that overlook the garden?

It is only November, and yet I am thinking about Christmas presents already. What is your father going to buy your mother? What is she buying him? What do you think you and your brothers and sisters will get?

Love from your friend,
Malcolm

P.S. I nearly forgot to ask. What is your dog's very favourite food?

Oliver handed the letter back to Nikhil.

'Extraordinary,' he declared. 'This continuing obsession with the small potatoes of other people's lives.'

'It's not extraordinary,' said Nikhil. 'I've been right round the class and looked. They're all like this. Endless silly boring questions.'

'In that case,' said Oliver, 'I'm truly grateful to have ended up with Simon Huggett.'

But though she could not put her finger on it exactly, something about the letter intrigued Laura.

'It's so peculiar,' she said. 'In places it sounds as if it wasn't written by a real person at all, but by a machine or a computer.'

'What do you mean?'

It was hard to explain quite what she did mean.

'Well,' she said. 'Try to imagine the person who wrote it.'

'*You* try imagining,' Nikhil said sourly. 'I've wasted enough of *my* time, writing.'

And stuffing the letter back in his jacket pocket, he ran off to play kickball with Chrissie and Kevin.

In the last few minutes before the bell rang for the beginning of school, Laura did try imagining Malcolm – some drab, whey-faced Sticklebury creature, interested principally in grades of deafness and grannies' bedrooms. But it wasn't easy. And her thoughts about Nikhil's penpal kept getting overshadowed by rather more uncomfortable reflections about her own, and Laura found herself imagining something infinitely more awful: that Miranda's response to Lady Melody's letter might, even now, be speeding closer and closer in a mailvan. Miranda had probably spent *hours* composing her reply to lonely and unhappy Lady Melody. Laura could just imagine it! She'd probably been as sensitive as she could about Lady Melody's father's sudden and shocking disappearance, and the family becoming penniless, and having to give up her precious ponies. Poor Laura groaned. Just thinking about it made her feel perfectly dreadful. Sweet-natured Miranda had probably sat at her own kitchen table, frowning with anxiety and nibbling the tip of her pen, trying to write a sympathetic letter to someone forced to go to a dismal new school where the teachers resented her noble title and a clumsy boy kept on jogging her elbow.

And it would be hard to think of what to write to someone as peculiar as Lady Melody – someone who wasn't even allowed to cheer herself up watching television because of the noxious rays that were bad for the body and the noxious programmes that were equally bad for the soul!

Hard? It would probably be *impossible*.

Laura stood in the leaf-strewn playground and blushed for shame. She felt sick right down to her scarlet rubber wellies. And she had only been *imagining* Miranda struggling to reply. How would she feel when a letter actually slid through the letter box at home, and landed at her feet?

She dreaded to think.

Oh, *why* hadn't she considered all this back in October, before it was too late? Because she'd been sticking her head in the sand, that's why, putting the problem out of her mind, not even telling Oliver about it. That was no way to sort out anything. You had to face your troubles head-on, and fight them properly or they would *never* go away.

She should have been brought up fearless, like Oliver. Oliver would have written directly, explaining exactly what had happened. He wouldn't still be in this terrible predicament, weeks later.

She had to think of something – fast!

The school bell rang out, loud and long. Miserably, Laura shuffled through the sodden leaves towards the double doors of the entrance. Everyone stamped with impatience, nudging one another in and out of line, until the doors were opened from the inside. Laura marched in straight past Mrs Coverley with her head down, still thinking hard, and had to be reminded to say good morning.

It didn't turn out to be a good morning, though. Quite the reverse. For some reason everyone was in a terrible mood. Even good friends were snarling at one another. Things were spilled, or mislaid, or broken. No one had the faintest idea what Mrs Coverley was on about when she tried to explain the work on the blackboard. And even the television programme was cancelled.

By eleven, the clammy mist beyond the windows had turned to such sharp, stinging rain that no one was allowed outside. And under the general relaxation of discipline that came along with indoor break, bad tempers very quickly turned into bad manners.

Mrs Coverley's cheerful suggestion that some of the class might spend their break writing letters to their penpals met with a barrage of criticism.

'My penpal's *useless*. I'm not writing to *her*.'

'She's not as boring as mine. She couldn't be!'

'Where did you get these penpals, anyway, Mrs Coverley?'

Mrs Coverley reflected. She was pinning up her thick pepper-and-salt hair for the third time that morning, before slipping off to the staffroom to fetch her coffee. When she replied it was indistinctly, through a mouthful of pins.

'I told you. I followed up an advertisement in *The Westburn Teacher*.'

'What did it say? "**TWENTY ONE BORING LETTER WRITERS SEEK FRESH PENPALS TO TORTURE**"?'

Mrs Coverley cautiously removed the last pin from between her teeth before putting on her dignified look and rebuking: 'Not at all. As I recall, it said something like: "**PACKS OF PENPALS FOR SCHOOL CLASSES. STATE AGES DESIRED. ALL FROM THE SAME TOWN TO ENCOURAGE PROJECT WORK**"'.

There was a common groan at the mention of projects.

'If I had to do any project work with that penpal of mine I'd die of boredom,' declared Jessica. Her lip curled, and she said in mincing tones: '"Our Old Sticklebury Cathedral has a font. Does your cathedral have a font?" I can just imagine what she would write!'

Imagine what she would write! Oh, not again! Reminded by the words, Laura felt quite queasy. She couldn't bear it.

And *wouldn't* bear it. Not a moment longer. And if the only way out of this tangle was to write to Miranda with a full explanation and an apology, she'd do it now, while she had time. Fearlessly.

Upending her desk lid, Laura rooted desperately inside. Note-paper. And a fairly clean envelope. Pen. Gazing out at the leaden sky for inspiration, she set herself to put things right.

> 21 Acacia Avenue
> Westburn

Dear Miranda,

She couldn't do it. Words wouldn't come.

Get that old pen moving! Laura gritted her teeth. Somehow her hand was moving across the paper. Only after a couple of paragraphs did she dare stop and read what she had written.

> So many things have happened to me since I last wrote that, even though I have not heard from you yet, I feel I must send another letter to keep you up to date.
>
> First, I have renounced my title so as to become a bit more normal and ordinary. This was a fancy ceremony which took a bit of time, so while I was at it I dropped a lot of my other names as well. And since I was teased terribly for being called Melody, I changed that too. To Laura. So now I am just plain Laura Irwin.

Well, it wasn't quite the explanation Oliver would have suggested. But Laura wasn't Oliver. And it was going to have to do.

Desperately, Laura pressed on.

> Then a quite amazing thing happened. The spacious set of rooms that was the third floor of our house was whipped off suddenly during a freak storm. And when my mother spoke to the builders afterwards, they told her the cheapest thing to do would be to put the roof back on top of the rooms underneath without bothering to rebuild the top floor. So we now live in a house with just an upstairs and a downstairs – a plain house on a plain street.

That's that, thought Laura, cheering up fast. Not only is it brilliant, but it helps with the next bit.

> So we have much less room than before. And mother decided that everything we didn't need should go, to make more space. So it was out with all the old French furniture, and the charming china and delicate glassware. To replace them, we have bought a normal grey sofa and two matching chairs, some mugs and plates from British Home Stores, and lots of assorted glasses like everyone else.

What else? What else? She mustn't miss out anything important.

> While she was at the dentist's a few days later, my mother happened to glance at a glossy magazine, and read that the problem with the noxious rays inside televisions has now been solved by Modern Science. When she mentioned this to the dental hygienist, he assured her that the programmes had also recently become very much better. So we went out and bought a television. It isn't new.

Amazing how fast one could write when one tried!

> And while we were sitting watching it one
> night, my mother saw a programme on
> poverty all over the world. She was so
> appalled to see the tatty rags some people
> were reduced to wearing, and their meagre
> meals, that she immediately rushed out and
> sold—

Sold what? Think back! She mustn't forget anything.

> the stuffed tigers' heads on the wall, and my
> father's collection of ivory snuff boxes, and
> the wine in the cellar and all the fancy knick-
> knacks and precious possessions,

Whoops! Nearly forgot!

> including all her priceless furs.

But she couldn't sell Grandmother's stuff, could she? Or Melody's? Not without asking. They'd have to decide that for themselves.

> So then she gave all the money to the Child
> Poverty Action Appeal and became a
> gardener. And I said I wanted to sell all my
> Chinese porcelain dolls, too, and I did. And
> when my grandmother heard, she was so very
> moved and touched, she at once sold all her
> jewels and even her beautiful huge mansion
> in the country, and moved to a little house
> in a fairly boring little street in a small town
> in Wales, where she now lives.

This was the difficult bit coming up.

> And a most astonishing and wonderful
> thing has happened,

Might as well kill two birds with one stone:

though it has its sad moments, too.

One day, while I was taking Czarina for a walk, she gave a sudden and excited yelp and, pulling the lead right out of my hand, she dashed straight across the road in front of a car.

This wasn't pleasant, but it had to happen.

She was killed outright. It was *entirely painless*.

What else might make Miranda feel better about it?

And she was very, very old. Ancient really. And rather rheumatic. Yes, I fear that Czarina's life had become a bit of a burden to her.

That should do nicely.

I knelt beside her in the street. And then the driver of the car got out and leaned over my shoulder, trying to comfort me. And I looked up and saw – I hope you don't find this too hard to believe – my own father! Yes! Truly amazing! Driving a green Ford Sierra through my own town! Found at last!

Press on quickly, before Miranda had time to become suspicious.

It turned out what happened all those months ago was that he bumped his head and got amnesia. So he forgot everyone and everything entirely, even his own name and where he lived! That's why we never heard a word.

But at the first sight of me, his only daughter, he suddenly remembered everything from before, just like that! And we fell into one another's arms, sobbing with relief and pleasure

Whoops! Mustn't forget poor Czarina!

as well as with sorrow, because of my poor
pet sprawled stone dead in the street.

Nearly there. Nearly there.

And while the vet was slipping Czarina's
mortal frame into a large green plastic bag,
she happened to mention to my father that
maybe I ought to have a new pet in order to
try to replace Czarina in my affections. So
we went into the nearest pet shop, and
bought a cat. They only had one that I really
liked. He was quite old and sluggish, but we
bought him anyway, and I have called him
Mr Whiskers. He feels quite at home already,
I think. Certainly he acts as if he has been
living in our house for years and years.

Right. That was that sorted out. Back to the
father.

And then my father drove us home in the
green Ford Sierra. He told me when he
couldn't remember who he was, he took a job
as a driver for this firm called Forrest Trade
Deliveries. Now he quite likes it, and would
like to carry on.

There. All done. Perfect.

And so, Miranda, see how everything has
changed. I now am plain old Laura Irwin,
and I live in a normal home with normal
things, and I have a perfectly normal mother
and father and granny and cat.

Thank God for that! And Laura finished with a
small, celebratory flourish.

And even the boy who sits next to me in class
has stopped jogging my elbow.
With love from,
Laura.

She lifted her head to meet a steely, unsmiling gaze boring at her through plastic lenses.

'At it again, are we?' enquired Oliver coldly.

Laura was appalled, simply appalled. It never occurred to her that he might be reading what she wrote over her shoulder.

Oliver still stared over the spectacles that had slid down his nose.

'You sent that Lady Melody letter after all,' Oliver accused her. 'That awful pack of lies. You posted it. Didn't you? *Didn't* you?'

But Laura had had a bad morning. And suddenly she had had more than enough of Oliver Boot's sanctimoniousness.

'No, I did *not*!' she snapped. 'So you can wipe that disapproving look off your face. My dad posted it. By mistake! Understand? It was a *mistake*!'

She spoke so crossly, Oliver was shocked. In his astonishment, his glasses slid off the end of his nose. Half-blind and desperate, he flailed his arms to catch them before they hit the floor and smashed. But it was Laura who deftly reached out and caught them.

'There you are!' she said, hurling them down on his side of the desk. 'Just make sure you use them to peer at things that are your own business, not mine!'

She turned her back on him, she was so angry. What sort of friend was it who immediately assumed the worst? A *rotten* friend. No friend at all.

Beside her, Oliver flushed scarlet. He, too, was furious. What sort of friend could keep the secret of a mistake like that from you? Not tell you what had happened day after day after day? A *rotten* friend. No friend at all.

The two shared a hostile silence. It lasted for the rest of the day. In the general cloud of ill-temper that hung about the classroom, nobody else noticed. No one came up, forcing a conversation that might have led to peace. Laura and Oliver spent the whole of the lunch hour avoiding one another. And when the bell rang for the end of the day, for the first time since term began they set off separately for home.

Laura walked on ahead. Oliver followed more slowly, scuffing the sodden mulch of leaves and kicking clumps of it aside as he walked. He didn't feel good about the quarrel. Not that you expect to feel good about a quarrel, exactly; but Oliver was at least used to feeling he was completely in the right. This time he didn't, and the whole business made him rather uncomfortable.

So Laura hadn't told him about the mistake. But why not? Maybe because he'd kicked up such a storm when, in all cheerful innocence, she'd written the first Lady Melody letter. He'd practically bitten her head off. And yet he knew that Laura was what Mrs Coverley always referred to as 'a sensitive plant'. Maybe he should have been a bit more careful about what he'd said, and how forcibly he'd said it.

Without realising what he was doing, Oliver speeded his pace a little.

A few yards ahead, Laura was feeling terrible. Oh, why had she been so snappy and horrid with Oliver? It wasn't his fault he'd been brought up to get in such a tizzy about these things! And it wasn't fair not to tell someone exactly what had happened, and then go and bite their head off when they misunderstood.

Unwittingly, she slowed her pace.

The two of them came together at the corner. Laura stopped for a bicycle that was miles away, and Oliver chose to cross at the very same place.

Oliver said:

'You must have felt awful when you realised the mistake.'

Laura shuddered at the memory.

'I couldn't bear thinking about it. That's why I never even told you.'

They fell in step together. After a few moments, Oliver said cheerfully:

'If you send this second letter, Miranda's going to think you lead a terribly exciting life.'

Beside him, Laura made a face.

'She's going to have such an exotic picture of you: all roofs torn off in storms, and disappearing fathers returning to the bosom of the family, and dying dogs, and giving up mink coats and aristocratic titles.'

Laura made a worse face. But Oliver persisted.

'She won't have a proper picture of you at all, will she?'

Laura turned her head to look suspiciously at Oliver, who'd turned his head to look at her.

'You're going to have to go down there,' he told her.

'Go down where?'

'Sticklebury, of course.'

Laura was horrified.

'But *why*?'

Oliver spread his hands with amazement that anyone could be so dense.

'To meet Miranda, of course! And put things right.'

'But I *have* put things right,' Laura argued desperately. 'I spent the whole of break writing this letter.'

Oliver shook his head.

'That letter doesn't put anything right, and you know it.'

Laura accepted defeat.

'No,' she agreed.

'*Lies must be thatched with more, or they rain through,*' Oliver quoted smugly.

'Oh, do stop, Oliver!' begged Laura. She was thinking hard. Go down to Sticklebury? It sounded quite impossible. But why not, after all? Her father drove that way every month, and he was used to taking Laura with him on weekends or school holidays. And if she met Miranda face to face, then she could – oh, no she couldn't.

'I *couldn't,* Oliver.'

'Of course you could.'

Oh, why wouldn't he go home and leave her alone! But instead of peeling off at the corner, Oliver now started accompanying Laura down her own street. Clearly he was determined to persecute her into submission.

'Why couldn't you?'

'I'd be scared stiff.'

'But why?'

Laura's face crumpled with anxiety as she attempted to explain. 'Because I don't *know* her, do I? I don't know anything about her except that

54

she's interested in microwave ovens and chest free-zers and food processors and stuff like that. How can I just appear on her doorstep one day and say: "Hello, I'm your penpal, Laura Irwin"? I couldn't do it. I would die of fright.'

'Let her know you are coming.'

'How?'

'Write her a letter.'

'Oh, Oliver!' In order to console herself, she scooped up a somnolent Mr Whiskers from where he lay stretched across the driveway, deeply asleep. 'No more letters, please!'

She spoke too soon. For when she lifted her face from Mr Whiskers' warm and throbbing fur, Oliver was pointing towards her front door. And there, protruding from the flap of the letter box, was one of Miranda's distinctive rainbow envelopes.

'Oh, *no*!'

She rushed up and snatched it from the letter box. She thrust it into Oliver's hand.

'*You* open it. I can't bear it.'

Oliver tore at the envelope. While Laura hugged her cat for comfort, he read aloud:

2A Cathedral Close
Sticklebury

My dear Lady Melody,
  How kind of you to write. I was so pleased to get your letter. And I am so sorry you are not very happy at your school. I never cared for mine much, either.

'Funny,' Oliver interrupted himself. 'Why "never cared for"? Has she left?'

'Just read it, quickly, Oliver,' pleaded Laura.

It is a pity you don't have a television set
to cheer you up. Or a video. Or a stereo. Or
a cassette record player. But never mind. We
must make do with what ~~you've~~ we've got.

'She's crossed the "you've" out and put
"we've",' explained Oliver.

'Get on with it,' begged Laura. '*Please.*'

And I can imagine you, Lady Melody, sitting
on your lovely old French furniture amongst
your charming china and delicate glassware.
But some things are a little more difficult to
imagine without help. For example, do your
grandmother's diamonds twinkle and glitter
in the lamplight? Or are all her precious
jewels safely locked away in the bank?

Oliver lowered the rainbow-coloured notepaper.

'Laura,' he said. 'There's something very fishy
indeed about this letter.'

'Read to the end, Oliver,' insisted Laura. 'Before
I scream.'

So Oliver pressed on.

Oh, Lady Melody, I simply *hate* to think of
you lying awake at nights, so lonely. Is dear,
dear Czarina allowed to sleep on your bed
and keep you company through the dark
hours? Or is she chained to a kennel, or shut
in the kitchen?

'Laura—'

'Just *read*, Oliver! *Read*!'

I was almost in tears when I read about
your father's sudden and shocking
disappearance. No doubt your mother and
grandmother, being so rich, will do their
very best to console you at Christmas. What
do you think they will do to try and brighten
up that sad little face? Maybe they'll buy you
a computer. Or do they have noxious rays,

56

too, like televisions? Perhaps you'll be given a radio cassette player. I shouldn't think getting – or, for that matter, losing – anything that's just large and expensive could ever matter two hoots compared with a father, or being happy at school, or having ponies. But that's just my personal opinion, of course.

Please write again, and answer all my questions, because I find I spend almost all my time thinking and wondering about you and your home.

Your friend,
Miranda

P.S. By the way, Lady Melody, what is your very favourite food? And what is Czarina's?

Oliver lowered the letter. Over it, Laura and he stared at one another uneasily. For both, snippets echoed disturbingly. Laura felt utter mortification as some of the sweet, kind things Miranda had written rang in her head:'I am *so sorry* you are not very happy at your school. . . . I simply *hate* to think of you lying awake at nights, so lonely. . . . I was almost in tears when I read about your father. . . . I spend almost all my time thinking and wondering about you and your family. . . .'

Oh, how could she ever explain to Miranda that not one word of her story was true?

Oliver was equally disturbed, but for completely different reasons. The echoes rang in his head, too: 'It is a pity you don't have a television set. . . . But we must make do with what you've we've got. . . . Are all her precious jewels safely locked away in the bank?. . . . Is Czarina chained to a kennel, or locked in the kitchen?'

Oh, there was certainly a lot more going on here

than something funny in the Sticklebury water!

Oliver peered at Laura. She looked pale and anxious. But maybe that was to be expected. She hadn't been brought up fearless like him and his sister. Oliver was determined not to make the same mistake twice. They had a job to do, but he must go gently. After all, Laura was a sensitive plant.

'Laura?'

She jumped as though startled out of a nightmare, and Mr Whiskers fled from her arms to the safety of the wall.

'Laura? About this ...' He didn't know quite how to put it. 'About this letter from Miranda. About this "penpal" of yours ...'

Laura stared at him, wide-eyed, so Oliver changed tack.

'Your father drives down to Sticklebury, doesn't he?'

Laura nodded.

'He goes every month.'

Oliver waited, but there was no response from Laura. So he pressed on.

'He's probably due to go down there again soon.'

Laura was silent.

'He fixes his own schedule, doesn't he? I mean, he could decide to go down to Sticklebury this Saturday, couldn't he? And take you with him? He often takes you with him at weekends when your Mum's working.'

Still Laura didn't speak.

Oliver spread his hands. There was no gentle way of putting it.

'Laura, I'm very much afraid that you're going to *have* to go down there.'

To his astonishment, Laura didn't even begin to argue. The expression on her face never changed. She simply drew the second Lady Melody letter out of her pocket – the letter filled with freak storms and reassuring dentists, with rheumaticky dogs and rediscovered fathers.

Slowly, calmly, as Oliver watched, she tore the letter into tiny pieces.

'You're quite right,' she agreed. 'I'm simply going to have to go down there.'

Nothing, not even the humiliation of standing on Miranda's doorstep trying to explain, could be worse than this guilt.

Oliver stared. This wasn't at all what he expected. Where was the tense and indecisive Laura that Mrs Coverley had put in the desk beside him? Had she turned fearless overnight?

'It might be difficult,' Oliver warned.

But Laura just shrugged. Thrusting the messy shreds of the letter into Oliver's hand, she scooped up her cat and made for her front door.

'See you tomorrow, Oliver,' was all she said.

Oliver stood gazing after her for a few moments, wondering. Then he glanced at the pieces of paper in his hand. On the way back to his own house he kept his eyes peeled for a litter bin. Of course, there were none. Only more of those Neighbourhood Watch signs that seemed to spring up like weeds after each fresh spate of burglaries in the town.

And all the way home he was thinking of Laura.

All the way down to Sticklebury Laura was thinking, too – of Miranda. The slim black wiper arms swept soothing arcs across the rain-stippled wind-screen. Her father settled into his usual comforting motorway drone – 'Saturday drivers . . . *far* too fast . . . find himself in a fog pocket and be sorry . . . don't like the look of that load – think maybe we'd better get past in a bit of a hurry' – and Laura found her thoughts drifting miles ahead.

'How far is it?'

'We've only just set off!'

'But how far is it? I just want to know.' (Want to know how long I have before I must stand there and confess.)

'About an hour and a half.' He flicked the wipers to a faster rhythm as rain fell more heavily. 'What time is this penpal of yours expecting you?'

'Expecting me?'

He glanced down, surprised by her surprise.

'I mean, what time did Miranda say you should come?'

Oh, no! Clearly he thought Miranda had invited her. And that, no doubt, was the reason he and Mum had so readily agreed to let her spend the morning in a strange town more than fifty miles from home. They had assumed the two penpals had planned this meeting together, by letter.

She couldn't let things fall through now. When would she get another chance to come? Not for weeks. What was it Oliver said? '*Lies must be thatched with more, or they rain through.*'

He was dead right, as usual.

Laura glanced surreptitiously at her watch. Nine thirty five. What had her father said? About an hour and a half?

'Eleven,' she lied firmly. 'Miranda's expecting

me about eleven.'

Now let's see Oliver Boot blame her for that one!

'She'll be lucky!' Mr Irwin had fallen back into his comfortable grousing. 'What with the jams on the ramp up to the ring road, and their daft one-way system round that crumbling heap.'

'What crumbling heap?'

'Sticklebury Cathedral.' He flashed his lights to let the lorry in front know it was safe to pull in. 'Should have pulled it down years ago, and built a nice new overpass.'

At the mere thought of Sticklebury's many and varied municipal planning failures, Mr Irwin relapsed into gloomy silence, punctuated solely by the occasional remark about other drivers' road sense, and the odd sour observation about all the signs expressing regret for inconvenience and delay caused by the road works.

Laura sat silent, fiddling a little nervously with the envelope in her hand. Oliver had given it to her to post on the way home from school the evening before. It was his reply to Simon Huggett's last letter. But Laura had walked straight past the pillar box, her mind filled with worries about Miranda. Really these penpals were an utter curse!

Laura looked down. The flap had practically come unstuck from all her fiddling. It can't, thought Laura, have been very good glue. Or maybe Oliver hadn't licked it properly. In any case, if she were to slip one tiny little finger in here. . . .

Whoops!

And what had Oliver found to say to Simon Huggett this time, anyway? How on earth had he managed to reply to all those quite extraordinary ravings about having head lice, and being Prince Charles' secret left-handed son, and being sent to the psychologist?

The windscreen wipers swathed perpetually. 'A really stupid place to overtake, that was,' muttered Mr Irwin. And silently, secretly, Laura slid Oliver's letter to Simon out of its envelope.

8 Green Lane
Westburn

Dear Simon Huggett,
    I hope you know you are a sad victim of everyone's inability to accept you just as you are. Your mother is doing you no favour in letting the school pack you off to the P-S-Y-C-H-O-L-O-G-I-S-T, and buying films for your camera behind your father's back. She would probably do better to let him give you a really good clip round the ear, like he wanted, and have done with the whole sorry boiling.

Extraordinary! You sit right next to someone for two whole terms, and you find out you don't know the first thing about what they're thinking!

    Nobody has the right to force you to pretend to be someone you are not by nature. If you are a clumsy, fidgety, awkward, fibbing truant then it is a great shame for your mother if that is not exactly what she wanted. But she should have another whisky and leave you alone, not try to get you changed into a calm and confident amateur photographer. If parents don't want surprises, and possibly very nasty ones, they shouldn't have babies of their own. They should choose a child they really fancy from all those without proper homes.

62

Laura's head spun with these unusual ideas.

'Dad,' she said. 'Do you like me exactly as I am?'

'One moment, love,' replied Mr Irwin. He was hunched forward, peering through the streaming windscreen. 'Just let me get us through this rather nasty stretch of contra-flow.'

> You are not ill, Simon Huggett, you are
> *odd,* and that is entirely different. And if you
> are not ill, then sending you to look at dots
> and draw pictures of your family is not
> medical treatment but grown-up bullying,
> and you should not put up with it.

Strong stuff! So these were the secret beliefs of her gentle, bespectacled desk companion – revolutionary Oliver Boot!

> And what about this camera they gave
> you? What happens when you get bored with
> it? Will everyone be sneakily watching,
> shaking their heads, wondering if you are
> losing your self-esteem and going to the bad
> again? What you do with your own free time
> is nobody's business. If they choose to punish
> you for skipping school, or telling lies, that's
> up to them. Fair enough. Rules are rules. But
> not having much self-esteem is not a crime.
> Laura, who sits beside me, has no confidence
> either. But her parents love her just as she
> is. They wouldn't dream of packing her off to
> be changed by a perfect stranger.

The huge blue arrows redirected them back into lane.

'What did you want, love?' asked Mr Irwin.

'It's all right,' Laura assured him. 'I know the answer now, thank you.'

> There are several more things I really
> think we ought to talk about. Why don't you

come for a visit? If your parents have managed to live with you for years, mine should be able to put up with one weekend of nail-chewing and twitching and squirming and fidgeting.

Yours most sincerely,
Oliver Boot

Well! Laura slid the letter back in its envelope and hastily sealed the flap, as though to try and prevent the strange new ideas inside it escaping. It certainly wasn't the sort of letter she'd like to receive. It was far too disturbing. She'd almost prefer Miranda's drivel about pink doors and microwave ovens. And how would poor Simon feel when he read it? Trying to imagine, she sat quite still, watching bare trees flick by in the rain until they reached the Sticklebury turning.

Even before they were anywhere near the town centre, Mr Irwin was working himself into a state about the traffic.

'Look at it! Saturday morning brings them out in *droves*. Can't they shop in the week? Lord knows where they all think they're going. Sticklebury has only one proper car park, you know.'

Sure enough, the streets round the Cathedral were jammed with lines of cars that barely moved. Laura's spirits sank at the thought of delay. It was like queuing for one's own execution.

Mr Irwin craned his neck to peer through his drop-mottled side window at the clock high on the cathedral tower.

'Ten past eleven already,' he said, and added doubtfully: 'Maybe I'd better just drop you off, and get on with my deliveries.'

'Why not?' Laura jumped at the idea. Even the

humiliation of confessing to Miranda couldn't be worse than this waiting. She should rush off, get it over with, get back, and *never* tell another lie.

'It'll be one of those narrow streets behind that great snarl-up,' her father told her.

'I'll slip out here, then, shall I?'

Before he could change his mind, she was out on the pavement.

'One o'clock!' called Mr Irwin. 'On the cathedral steps. I'll hoot twice, loudly. And you will have to be quick. I won't be able to stop for more than a moment, you know. You'll practically have to throw yourself in.'

Laura caught the last drift of his complaining as he pulled out of the stationary line of cars, and turned back towards the outskirts. 'Of course, if the council had only had the courage and foresight. . . .'

Somehow, hearing the tail end of this familiar litany made the strange town seem just a shade less alarming. But Laura felt wretched enough as she stepped over the fast-flowing rivulets in the gutter, and set off through the downpour to find Miranda.

'Cathedral Close?' The passers-by looked puzzled. 'Not sure that – oh, of course! The alley right along the west wall!'

Left, right, then second left. Laura followed instructions. The streets were narrow and short, and within minutes she was standing beneath a sign that said: CATHEDRAL CLOSE.

But which of these houses was Miranda's? None of them seemed to have proper names or numbers. It was a strange, dark alley, so narrow she could see only a strip of sky overhead. Every few feet along on either side there was a door or a window.

Presumably Sticklebury postmen knew who lived in each of these dwelling places in the very shadow of the cathedral, but Laura was baffled.

Hold on a minute, though!

> My house has four pink windows and one pink door. I think pink is a very nice colour, don't you?

Right, then. That was clear enough. Laura trailed up and down the whole length of the alley, avoiding the puddles, looking for four pink windows and one pink door. Disconcertingly, there were none to be seen, though she checked both sides twice. The most she found was one mud-coloured window frame which might, she thought, if you looked on it favourably during a sunset, have had a bit of a pinkish tinge to the woodwork.

But sunset could never reach down here.

Bells chimed high overhead. Half past eleven! The time crept on, but she was getting nowhere. Laura swung round, searching for any clue at all, any name, any number. And over a crooked little porch she noticed an ancient, rusting iron plate.

## THE HERMITAGE

Now wasn't that familiar? Desperately, Laura scoured her memory. The Hermitage. Where had she seen it written before?

Of *course*! Nikhil's penpal! It was the address at the top of his letters. And what was his name? Not much more memorable than his letters, probably; but surely she could remember.

Malcolm. Yes, that was it. Malcolm.

Malcolm would know which house was Miranda's. You couldn't live in an alley as short as this, and not know everyone else, at least by sight. Malcolm would point her in the right direction. And if he wasn't home, his parents would help.

Laura stepped into the porch. It was a relief to be out of the rain, if only for a few moments. She shook the glistening drops off her hair and wiped her wet face with her sleeve. Then, desperately hoping someone was in, she reached towards the little bell set in the door above the letter box.

And noticed something really quite odd.

Laura withdrew her finger from the bell without pressing it. Pushing her damp hair back from her face, she peered more closely at what she'd seen, tucked away on the porch wall.

A little cardboard sign, no bigger than a visiting card.

*Mail for*
*2A–2S Cathedral Close*

Laura stared. Mail for 2A–2S Cathedral Close – printed quite clearly in black and white. Did Miranda live here, then? Along with Malcolm and, it seemed, plenty of others? Laura pressed her chilled fingertips against the seam of her jeans, counting the number of letters between A and S. If none were missed out, there were nineteen. Add on the original old name of THE HERMITAGE and behind this rickety porch you had twenty addresses.

Ridiculous.

Laura stepped back into the alley. *Four pink windows and one pink door. I think pink is a very nice colour, don't you?* There was only one window high up beside this porch, and it had certainly not been pink in years. Ivy was growing up one side. No one could have painted the window frame recently without doing some damage to the creeper. In any case, around the window's filthy glass panes, the drab green paint was flaking with age. Paint on the sill beneath was peeling badly. Bare wood showed through in several places. And there was not a sign of pink.

There couldn't be any more windows at the back, either. All of the buildings on this side of the alley were joined to the cathedral wall. *Four pink windows and one pink door.* What kind of liars were these Sticklebury folk?

Suddenly a shadow moved across the neglected window. Someone was moving on the other side. Hastily, Laura stepped back and flattened herself against the alley wall between the creeper and the porch. She didn't want to be caught peering suspiciously through Miranda's window.

Suspiciously? Yes, suspiciously. She couldn't help it. It was because Miranda had lied. It might be a stupid little falsehood – what did it matter how many windows were set in a wall or what colour they were painted? No one would like Miranda more, or less, for having five scarlet windows, or only one green one. But it was a lie, and trust was gone. From now on, how would Laura ever be sure which of the things Miranda wrote were truth and which were lies? How could you ever depend on someone's word again, once you had found them out for a liar?

But, then again, Miranda hadn't said much about herself, had she? That was what made her such a grisly penpal. She never told you anything about her life, or her home, or her friends. Not like Simon

Huggett, who, once he started, couldn't staunch the steady flow of intimate confidences; or Oliver, who'd even taken to comforting Simon with details of Laura's little habits and weaknesses.

No, 'four pink windows and one pink door' apart, Miranda tended to stick to her questions. She had shown sympathy for Lady Melody in her last letter, to be fair; but even that quickly turned into more boring enquiries. 'What do you think your mother will buy you to try and brighten up that sad little face at Christmas? A computer?' No, all Miranda was really interested in was large expensive things.

Large, expensive things. . . .

Lies go hand-in-glove with other forms of wrong-doing, don't they? You don't need lies to shore up honesty and fairness. Good people don't go round telling giant whoppers – there's simply no need. The only people who depend on lies to get by are people like murderers and cheats and thieves. . . .

Cheats and thieves. . . .

Thieves. . . .

Was it possible? What was it Oliver had said? 'Laura, there's something very fishy indeed about this letter.' At the time, she'd been too wrapped up in worrying about Miranda to pay him any attention. But Oliver was so keen to get her down to Sticklebury. He *must* have suspected something. And he must have thought she was suspecting the same. Well, he was wrong. She hadn't bargained for this at all. The very possibility that penpal Miranda, just like Lady Melody, was not exactly who she claimed to be, came as a great shock and surprise to Laura.

And.... And?

And as a great relief. Yes. If she admitted it to herself, a relief. Why else should she begin to feel her courage returning and her spirits rising, just like a condemned prisoner who hears the word 'reprieve' spoken outside his cell, just like a skylark suddenly freed from a bird-cage – like Laura herself, before all this miserable business began. Was it really and truly possible that Miranda could turn out to be even worse than a liar? That, for the first time in weeks, Laura could give up feeling so horribly, horribly guilty?

She had to know. Even if it were difficult, or dangerous, she couldn't let slip this one and only chance. There was the window, and she had to look.

Rain dripped from rotting eaves, unnoticed, on Laura's head. Keeping her back to the wall, she edged imperceptibly sideways, hoping that anyone who looked out of a window or passed by would simply assume she was leaning against the alley wall, waiting for someone.

No one came by. Nobody noticed.

She kept moving stealthily sideways until she stood once again behind the thick stem of the creeper. One quick look up and down the wet alley, and Laura was sliding her fingertips over the peeling paintwork, and lifting herself up on her toes to peer inside.

Away on the far side of the room, a balding man in a faded green corduroy jacket stood with his back to the window. He was, it seemed, having some difficulty refilling his pen from one of a forest of ink bottles on top of a grey filing cabinet. As Laura furtively pushed aside the waxy leaves of ivy in order to get a better look, his pen slipped from his hand, and droplets of bright purple ink spattered the metal drawers of the cabinet. Clearly his shirt was spattered too, for, as Laura watched, the man pulled it out from his trousers, inspected it with impatience and strode from the room.

Free from the risk of being seen, Laura drew herself higher on her toes and, resting her chin on the window sill, took a good long look.

The room looked dank and cheerless – not like a home at all, more like a storeroom. Along one wall were stacked piles of cartons. Some had handwritten labels: **Mitsumi Colour Television. Audio Four-speaker Stereo. Quikcook Microwave. Task Home Computer.** All large, expensive things.

And on a table directly beneath the window were several notebooks and a calendar, and a huge assortment of pens and pencils jammed in an old cake tin. There were piles of letters in office baskets. The nearest basket had been labelled *In*; the middle one said *Out*; the third *Now File*. Each basket was filled to overflowing. And right in front of them, flat on the table, lay a half-finished letter written in exactly the same shade of purple with which the balding man had so much trouble filling his pen.

You didn't sit in a double desk day after day without learning how to read sideways and upside down.

Dear Zafira,
  I was so glad to get your letter. I should be very interested indeed to know what you are

getting for Christmas. You don't have a
computer yet, do you? Why don't you ask for
one of those? Or you could ask for a

Here, the letter ended abruptly. The writer had
run out of purple ink!

Laura's toes ached with the effort of peering over
the sill. But just as she was about to let her weight
back on her heels and step out of sight behind the
creeper stem, she noticed one last thing, something
she recognised, something of hers. Something so
entirely conclusive that there was no need to look
any further.

Tossed in a wire basket, clipped to a few blank
sheets of the distinctive rainbow-coloured notepaper Laura had come to associate with Miranda,
was the very first Lady Melody letter!

So.

Laura let herself down and leaned flat against the
cold, wet wall. Rain fell on her in sheets from the
eaves above, but she didn't notice.

There wasn't any Miranda. No, nor any
Malcolm. And no Philip. The whole pack of
penpals, twenty names, boiled down to one great
big liar. No Miranda. Just a balding man in a faded
green corduroy jacket who'd had the cunning idea
of placing fraudulent advertisements in teaching
magazines, and writing to his prospective victims
for information:

Is your Granny deaf? Do your whole family
ever go out together in the evenings? What
is your dog's very favourite food?

Neighbourhood Watch signs can spring up all
over. This burglar won't notice. He's here, a couple
of hours drive away, stacking his loot into boxes,

and sorting out the last few snippets of information he needs for his next rash of robberies.

But no Miranda. There was *no Miranda*! Laura couldn't help bursting into smiles. If anyone notices me, she thought, standing here leaning against the wall in the pouring rain, grinning like a jackass, they'll think I'm mad.

But why hadn't anybody realised? They'd noticed the letters were so tedious that almost everyone was desperate to swap. And she herself had argued that the letter from Malcolm could just as well have been written by a computer. Why hadn't anyone gone round the class, looking? They would have noticed at once that all the addresses were suspiciously alike.

Because the letters were so dull, that's why. People could scarcely bring themselves to read to the end of their own, let alone other people's. And if they thought anything at all, it was: However Am I Going To Reply To This Drivel?

The only person in the class who might have checked things out was Oliver. And he had, by sheer chance, landed the only real penpal in the whole bunch – Simon Huggett. 'I have been forced to write to you,' he'd said in his very first letter. Forced to volunteer by his aunt because he lived in Sticklebury too, and Mrs Coverley needed one more name. Simon. The only penpal in the whole pack who had a spark of life in him.

She'd thought that he was mad. He was just *real*.

'Pssst!'

What was that?

Laura turned in the direction of the noise. But there was no one in the alley, no sign of movement, except for a pale lemon curtain billowing from a window a few houses down.

'Pssst!'

Was somebody trying to catch her attention? Again Laura's head turned, but during the couple of seconds she was distracted, there was a rattle and a click right behind her, and, when she turned back, the man in the faded green corduroy jacket was backing out of the rickety porch, a folded newspaper tucked under his arm.

He seemed a little surprised to see Laura standing in driving rain beside his porch.

'Looking for someone?' he asked.

She could say yes, she could say no. But she found that she couldn't say either because her voice had quite deserted her.

'Well?' There was impatience in his tone. It was, after all, an extremely wet place to be kept waiting.

Still Laura couldn't speak. It wasn't as if he looked dangerous, or even unpleasant. It was the awful business of knowing he was a liar and a thief while he thought she had simply strayed by accident into the alley. She was sure he might read her thoughts – find her out!

'I—'

'What?' He was really impatient now. 'Who *are* you? What are you *doing* here? Where do you *live*?'

Laura's whole body stiffened. She couldn't tell him that she came from Westburn. That would make him suspicious at once. But she had to think of something, and very quickly.

In her anguish, her hands clenched tight inside her jacket pocket. And as they did so the fingers of her left hand closed round stiff paper.

Oliver's letter. Of course!

Hastily Laura drew it from her pocket.

'I'm lost,' she announced.

'Lost?'

'Yes. I have a letter to deliver.'

She held it up, hoping he wouldn't notice she'd spread her thumb over the stamp. A huge drop of water fell from the eaves and splashed on the crumpled envelope, blurring half Simon Huggett's name.

The man held his folded newspaper over the letter to protect it. Narrowing his eyes, he read the address on the envelope.

'You're not lost,' he contradicted her firmly. 'You're here.'

Laura looked down. Simon's address was clear enough: 17, Cat Alley, Sticklebury.

'But this street's called Cathedral Close.'

'And that's Cat Alley.'

Laura looked up, astonished. Under the newspaper he was using as an umbrella, the man was grinning at her confusion.

'That's what it's called,' he assured her. 'By everyone. Only the postmen use the proper name. For all the rest of us it's Cat Alley, and has been for hundreds of years.'

So that's why everyone she asked had looked puzzled.

Now he was checking the number again.

'So if it's number seventeen you want, then let me see. Mrs Hughes over there is number eleven. And the numbers rise as you walk along that way....'

As he went on, working it out for her, Laura

risked peeping up at his face. It wasn't, she realised, a disagreeable face at all. In fact, he looked really quite pleasant and friendly. The way he was holding the newspaper more over her than over himself was very generous in the circumstances. And the way he was droning on amiably even reminded her a bit of her own father: 'So I reckon if that's number fifteen, which it must be, then you must want that house over there – the one with that pale lemon curtain flapping from the upstairs window.'

To her astonishment, as he finished speaking he laid a hand on her shoulder and gently propelled her along the alley.

'If you were mine, I wouldn't want you hanging about like a drenched kitten. Let's get on and deliver your letter, young lady, and see you safely out of this downpour.'

She prayed he'd abandon her at Simon's door and go off on his own errand. She hoped she might stand quietly on the doorstep for a moment or two, till he was out of sight, then slip away and post the letter in the next pillar box she passed. The last thing she wanted was to deliver this little bombshell personally. But to her horror, when they reached the house he stopped, and stood behind her, holding the newspaper over her head.

She had no choice but to tap on the door.

'More of a mouse's scrabble than a knock,' he scoffed. 'That won't do, will it?'

He reached over her and banged on the door as though intending to raise the dead.

'There,' he said. 'That should do nicely. They must have heard that.'

And, in an instant, he was gone, leaving the

newspaper draped over her head.

Laura's first instinct was to flee before the thunderous knock was answered. But just as she pulled the damp paper off her hair, the door swung open.

There, towering above her, stood Simon Huggett.

Even if he had not been gripping a camera tightly to his chest, there would have been no mistaking him. The fingernails gave it away at once. They looked more gnawed than bitten, Laura thought. He wasn't squirming or twitching, though. Perhaps he'd improved a bit lately. He was astonishingly tall. 'Taller than average' he had said of himself. In fact, he was a good head and a half taller than Laura, and she was not small for her age. Part of her was tempted to peep at his huge feet, but in the end nerves and good manners prevailed.

'Good morning,' said Simon after his own few moments of silent staring. 'Are you going round collecting?'

Defeated, Laura held out the letter.

'Here,' she said. 'This is for you. From Oliver Boot.'

Simon looked astonished. His hand reached out and took the letter, but not for a moment did he stop watching Laura.

'Have you come all the way from Westburn to deliver it?' he asked incredulously.

Laura hadn't the energy to embark on an explanation. She simply nodded. Suddenly she felt tired and drained and miserable, and wished with all her heart she could be back in Westburn now, in her own home, with her mother and father clattering around making her feel safe, and Mr Whiskers in her arms.

Perhaps Simon Huggett sensed her rising distress.

'You're terribly wet,' he told her. 'Why don't you come in?'

Laura looked at her watch. It wasn't even twelve o'clock yet. She hadn't wanted to be there when Simon read his letter from Oliver Boot, but there was more than an hour to go before she'd be rescued from this strange and horrible town by her father. And rain was still bucketing down as if the seas, and not the skies, were overhead and overflowing.

'All right,' she said. And then, trying to sound a little less ungracious: 'Thanks very much.'

'My mother has a hair drier you can use,' said Simon.

He stepped back, making way for Laura, who tucked the wet newspaper under her arm and followed him inside the house, watching him as he started up the stairs. He climbed them in the most extraordinary fashion – crab-wise, with hands spread on the walls, and dangerous leanings over the bannisters. Laura couldn't for the life of her think what he was about until she realised he was trying to avoid the yellow swirly bits of the carpet.

So he wasn't quite normal yet, then. Not completely.

She stared, fascinated, as he made his slow progress upwards.

'There!' he called down with no small satisfaction on reaching the landing.

She could see why he was so proud of himself.

The ascent hadn't looked at all easy.

As Laura followed up the stairs in a more normal fashion, Simon drew a small plastic hair drier from a drawer in a wooden chest, and plugged it in a socket beside the mirror on the landing wall. Switching it on, he handed it to Laura, who perched on the edge of the chest, and, lowering her head, let the warm, noisy rush of air sweep her wet hair across one side of her face.

Out of the corner of her other eye, she watched Simon Huggett warily as he ripped open the envelope and started reading Oliver's letter. He didn't look any too pleased about what he found in it. From behind the shelter of her drying hair, Laura saw his eyes flash and narrow, and his lips thin.

'He thinks I need a good clip round the ear more than a camera!' he shouted angrily above the buzz of the drier.

'I'm sure that's not *exactly* what he says,' Laura rebuked Simon gently.

'Well, he definitely calls me a clumsy, fidgety, awkward, fibbing truant!'

Anxious as she was to defend Oliver, there was no denying this, so Laura kept silent.

'He wants to talk to me, so he's invited me to Westburn. He reckons his family should just about be able to bear me for a couple of days!'

'I think,' Laura picked out her words with care, 'he feels he might be able to be helpful.'

'Helpful! I don't think he's likely to be at all helpful! Oh, no! In fact, I think that your Oliver Boot is far more likely to turn out to be a rude and meddling *idiot*!'

He spoke with tremendous force. He sounded

79

positively livid. Pushing her damp hair back from her face, Laura politely switched off the hair drier in order to listen to the tirade that followed.

'I've never read such a horrible letter! How *dare* he? Making my mother out to be some sort of idiot who doesn't even know what's best for me! She knows me a good deal better than he does!'

'I'm sure she does,' soothed Laura.

'He's all brains and no sense, your Oliver Boot. He doesn't know what he's talking about. I *like* my new camera. I really do! I've always wanted one, and my mum knew it. I've spent *days* working out how to use it. I can do pretty complicated things with it now.'

'I'm sure you can.'

'And I feel a lot better about things now, too. We all do. I like the psychologist. She's very nice. And she's been very helpful. She's done things that nobody else could, not even my mother. She's even stopped my father going on and on at me about being no good at games, and liking Little Peter next door so much, and wanting to give up my evening paper round in the middle of winter.'

Laura felt a real rush of sympathy for Simon when she heard this. She'd always thought paper rounds must be dreadful in winter – all that cold and wet and dark, the traffic fumes and noise, and the irritable, home-going people.

'When I told her how I felt about all those things, she invited my dad in to a session, and told him where to get off.'

'Did she *really*?'

'Well, not exactly in those words. But he knew perfectly well what she meant!'

'I bet he did!'

All Laura's nervousness about Simon Huggett had disappeared. She was fascinated with him and his story.

'So things are better now. Much better. And I don't like getting a letter like this from a penpal who barely knows me. It's so cocky and *smug*.'

'Oh, yes,' said Laura. 'Oliver Boot is smug.'

It was, she thought, the main danger with being fearless. You never feared you might be wrong.

She switched the hairdrier back on as Simon started off again, pointing out even more of Oliver Boot's shortcomings. Just like his letters, he went on a bit. Her curiosity concealed behind a hedge of drying hair, Laura looked about her with growing interest.

It was a tidy house, far tidier than her own home. The carpet looked freshly vacuumed, and all except one of the doors on the landing were neatly closed. Was that room Simon's? Through the half-open door she could see posters on the wall, a rumpled candlewick bedspread covered with black and white photographs – and pale lemon curtains billowing over the sill!

Was it Simon, then, who had been calling 'Pssst!' at her out of his window? But why should he try to attract a perfect stranger's attention in that way? Was *everyone* in Sticklebury mad or bad?

Her eyes dropped to the damp back page of *The Sticklebury Herald* lying beside her on the chest. One hour in the town, and she would not have been in the slightest surprised to find a headline: **WEIRD CHEMICAL FOUND IN CITY WATER SUPPLY.**

But what she did see was even stranger. It was a blurred newspaper photograph of a man with a thick stocking over his head. He was staggering into a shop carrying two cardboard cartons, and underneath was written:

### Baffling Benefactor Bestows Bounty

Intrigued, Laura tilted the drier to blow her hair away from her eyes. With Simon's continued grumbling entirely muffled by the buzz of the drier in her ears, she read on.

> Yesterday the masked man all Sticklebury charity shop organisers hope will drop in on them made surprise visits to several of the charity shops along Ballspond Road.
>
> 'Though oddly-dressed, he was charming,' insisted Red Cross Lady Mrs Urquhart (56). 'He even refused to allow me to carry his carton on the grounds that I might strain myself.'
>
> Equally impressed was Ms Linda Hastings, (26), from the Oxfam shop a few doors down. 'Mystery Man or not, he is welcome here any time,' she told the Herald. 'We can sell anything he leaves.'
>
> In yesterday's rash of short visits Sticklebury's baffling benefactor left behind him a video machine, a pair of electric hedge-clippers, a microwave oven and an Expresso coffee-maker, all in good working order.

So. A Mystery Man. A Baffling Benefactor. He did take other people's things – but then he gave them all away again! He'd seemed so pleasant – and perhaps he was. He was a sort of modern Robin Hood!

But he was still a thief.

Laura switched off the hairdrier to catch the next few words of Simon's harangue:

'... be so complacent and patronising about a person he knows nothing about!'

'Simon,' she interrupted the flow. A plan was hatching fast in her mind – a complicated and ambitious plan for which she would need his cooperation. 'Simon, it's no use going on and on about poor Oliver. You're just going to have to come to Westburn and meet him.'

Simon said sulkily:

'I don't see why. I know already that I won't get on with him.'

'That's not the point,' said Laura. 'The point is, we need you.'

'Need me?'

'Yes. Oliver and I need your help.'

He threw his hands up in the air.

'Why me? Why *me*?'

'*You*,' Laura said, 'because living almost exactly opposite your house is Sticklebury's Baffling Benefactor – the man who is robbing all the houses in Westburn!'

And before rushing back to the Cathedral steps to meet her father as the clock chimed one, Laura explained the whole business to an astonished Simon Huggett.

# ★ December ★

The harsh December sunlight poured through the classroom window. Unmercifully, it highlighted each smeary fingerprint, each smudge of dirt, each blemish in the glass. Laura shielded her eyes against the glare as Oliver read aloud the final version of the Lady Melody letter that they'd been working on together in snatched moments over the last few days.

'There! What do you think?'

'Perfect!'

'It *is* good, isn't it?'

'I'll copy it out.'

She rooted through the crêpe paper and tinsel and spilled glitter inside her desk, searching for writing paper. It was that stage in the winter term when Mrs Coverley took full advantage of her class's passion for making seasonal decorations, and spent a few uninterrupted moments filling in their reports. Knowing full well what she was doing up there at her desk, the class behaved just like the angels they were cutting out and pinning and gluing. There was only the softest burble of borrow and lend above the rustle of paper and snipping of scissors, as Laura copied the letter out neatly.

> 21 Acacia Avenue
> Westburn

'I'm not jogging your elbow too much, I hope,' Oliver murmured in mock concern. He was making a reindeer sleigh out of four toilet rolls and an old yoghurt carton.

Laura grinned, and kept writing.

Dear Mr Penpal,
   May I call you that? For I can hardly call
you Miranda any more – not now I know
that you are really just a middle-aged man in
a green corduroy jacket, with an ink-spotted
shirt and a bald head.

'You're *sure* it's not too rude . . .?'

'It is the truth,' Oliver declared, a little too
sanctimoniously.

'Truth can be very rude indeed,' said Laura. And
without further discussion she took it upon herself
to scratch out 'bald head' and write in its place
'receding hairline'.

'Oh, well,' said Oliver. 'At least this way he
won't be too offended to carry on reading.'

   And I know, too, that you are a thief. I
know you could say that a Baffling
Benefactor who Bestows Bounty on worthy
charities is not a *real* thief. But try telling
that to the people who worked hard and saved
up and paid for the videos and stereos and
microwave ovens you have stolen. You would
not be likely to get contented nods of
agreement.

'More likely to get a black eye and a thick ear,'
Oliver said.

   People prefer to choose for themselves
which of their household belongings they'll
give to charity. So I doubt if your generosity
to the needy will save you from going to
prison if you are arrested.

'This is the good bit coming up,' said Laura.

Oliver stopped snipping delicately round his
yoghurt carton and watched as she copied out the
next sentence in block capitals.

88

**AND ARRESTED YOU WILL CERTAINLY BE –
IF YOU PERSIST IN THIS THIEVING!**

'That's the stuff,' he murmured. 'Go to it, Lady
Melody!'

> Imagine my horror when I came, in all good
> faith, to visit my dear, sweet, supportive
> friend Miranda! Who did I see?

'It really ought to be "whom",' Oliver grumbled
quietly.

'Don't be silly,' said Laura. 'We've been through
this. No one writes "whom" any more. *No one.*'

> Who did I see? *You!* In your thief's den with
> your ill-gotten gains! A barefaced robber!
> (No stocking over your head then!) And all
> your stolen goods neatly set out and labelled!
> And all the evidence of your many forgeries
> spread over your table – including my letter
> to Miranda! How dare you? How *dare* you?
> You are a thief, a liar and a cheat!

'He looked so nice,' said Laura. 'And he was
very helpful. I can't believe he's really bad.'

'Softie!' scoffed Oliver. 'Good thing your Lady
Melody has more grit than you!'

> But though I myself could never take what
> belongs to another, don't think I came away
> from your house empty-handed. You can see
> that I have—

She hesitated. The word she was copying was
nothing but a thick, black smudge on the page.

'I-N-C-O-N-T-R-O-V-E-R-T-I-B-L-E,' Oliver offered
kindly.

'Thank you,' said Laura.

incontrovertible proof you are up to no
good. Ignore it at your peril. And do not
bother to destroy it – I have copies. And I will
not hesitate to give this proof to the police
if I should ever suspect you are up to your
tricks again. And I would know at once,
believe me. Because a good friend of mine
(you couldn't imagine who it is) will be
keeping an eye on you from now on. If one
single hair on my head comes to harm, you
will naturally be the first suspect!

'Bit late for you, though,' Oliver observed.

'You keep forgetting,' said Laura, 'this man is
*nice.*'

Don't think you would escape the long arm
of the law of the land. For my uncle is the
Chief of Police, you know. And the Lord
Chancellor has been absolutely devoted to
my mother since he fell tragically in love
with her on Westminster Cathedral steps a
few moments after she married my dear
father.

She started on the last page.

I hope you will not feel nasty and vindictive
about this. Theft is theft, after all, and this is
a fair cop. You stop at once, and I won't tell
anyone what you've done – ever. Keep your
side of the bargain and I'll keep mine.

Laura chewed on her pen.

'There's one more little thing,' she said. 'I'll slip
it in here.'

Oliver watched over her shoulder with interest
as she added one extra paragraph they hadn't dis-
cussed.

And I assure you I am not in the slightest
put out about losing my penpal. Miranda's
letters were so appallingly dreary that her
sudden end has come very much as a relief.

'Now that *is* rude,' said Oliver.

'It is the truth,' Laura insisted firmly.

She finished the letter.

> And now it only remains for me to take this opportunity to wish you every happiness in the coming season of good cheer.
>> Yours very sincerely,
>>> Lady Melody Estelle Priscilla Hermione Irwin.

Laura laid down her pen.

'There!'

She waited for Oliver to chime in 'Perfect!'. But he was silent. He was staring abstractedly out of the window and over the frost-coated bike shed into the silver sunlight.

'Oliver?' she asked anxiously.

Oliver sighed.

'What's the matter?'

He shrugged.

'Oh, come on, Oliver. Tell me,' Laura persisted.

Oliver made a face.

'It's the letter. It *worries* me.'

'In case it doesn't work?'

To her relief, Oliver brushed this idea aside at once. 'No, not that.'

He paused.

'Well?' Laura prompted.

'Don't you *see*?' Oliver burst out. 'This letter's just another pack of lies!'

'Not *just* another, Oliver. It's for a good reason.'

Oliver shook his head.

'But don't you see, Laura, that that's exactly what our burglar would say about what *he's* been doing! That since it's all in a good cause, it isn't really wrong. But maybe it is.'

'But he is stealing. And we're only telling a few tiny fibs.'

' "Only"!' scoffed Oliver. ' "A few tiny fibs"! See how you're even having to choose your words to try and hide the fact that it's *wrong*.'

'Oh, honestly, Oliver!'

There were times when Laura Irwin had no more patience with Oliver Boot, and this was one of them. In her opinion, he was far, far too clever for his own good.

'Simon Huggett's quite right about you, Oliver,' she told him acidly. 'You're all brains and no sense!'

In her exasperation, she let her voice rise sharply above the angelic murmurings in the classroom and catch Mrs Coverley's attention.

Mrs Coverley lifted her head.

'*What* did you say, Laura Irwin?'

Laura flushed scarlet.

'Nothing,' she muttered.

But Mrs Coverley was curious.

'Oh, yes,' she insisted. 'I heard you. But I'm not sure I made out the exact words.'

Laura hung her head.

'I just told Oliver he's all brains and no sense.'

'Oh!'

Mrs Coverley was astonished. Hastily she lowered her head before anyone could notice the broad smile of amusement that spread across her face. But she couldn't help relishing the brief exchange. And when she came to the REMARKS section of Laura Irwin's report, she wrote after a moment's reflection:

'I'm glad to see that some of the confidence of those around her is finally rubbing off on Laura. Of course, it is still to be hoped that some of her sensitivity will rub off on others...'

Meanwhile, behind his toilet roll sleigh, Oliver was pursuing his case with some vigour. As usual, he was more interested in the issue itself than in the insult he had suffered.

'It could be argued,' he said, 'That a liar, being a liar himself, has no right to get on his high horse if someone lies right back at him – especially in self-defence.'

'Right!' Laura said briskly. 'That sounds pretty watertight. Why don't we simply argue that, then?'

'*But*,' Oliver persisted, pointing his yoghurt carton at Laura. 'There are our own consciences to be considered. Do we really want to blot them by mixing ourselves up in deceit, for however good a reason?'

'I don't mind blotting mine,' Laura generously offered. 'It's a bit blotty anyway, after that first Lady Melody letter.'

'But what about me? Just going along with something you know is wrong is quite as bad as doing it yourself.'

'Not *quite* as bad, surely?' Laura pleaded.

'As close as makes no difference,' declared Oliver sternly.

'You are so difficult, Oliver,' Laura sighed. 'You're really *very awkward indeed*.'

'I'm not deliberately awkward,' Oliver defended himself. 'It's just that I can't help worrying about these things.'

Laura impatiently raised her eyes to heaven as

he went on, fretting gently:

'If we start lying, too, there'll be more lies about, won't there? And the more lies there are about, the less everyone in the world is going to be able to trust one another.'

Laura was barely listening. She was busy addressing a huge, brown envelope she'd brought from home.

'It would be horrible if no one could trust anybody any more,' Oliver rambled on. 'And if even *honest* people like us start finding reasons and excuses for telling lies—'

Laura was sticking a stamp on the envelope now. She wasn't listening at all.

'Then things would get worse and worse. Soon no one would be able to trust anyone. Life would become simply intolerable.'

Laura opened the envelope and slid Lady Melody's letter inside.

'There!' she interrupted him. She was brutal and firm. 'Finished at last. And just as soon as Simon comes up trumps with the proof, I'm going to post it.'

To her astonishment, the agonised look all over Oliver's face cleared instantly to sunny calm.

'Oh, well,' he said, going back to snipping neatly at his reindeer sleigh. 'If you're determined to persist with this, no matter how wrong it is, then there's no more to be said, is there?'

'No,' Laura responded drily. 'I suppose there isn't. So why don't you put down that ridiculous, messy sleigh, and get on with the letter to Simon Huggett?'

Oliver looked at his sleigh with a dispassionate

eye. It *was* a bit of a mess, he had to admit. He couldn't have been concentrating on it at all. It didn't even look like a reindeer sleigh. It looked more like an old, battered dustbin trolley.

He crumpled it up in his hands, and shoved it out of sight inside his half of the desk.

'Righty-ho,' he agreed, picking up his pen. 'Action stations. Laura's Great Plan is under way. Full steam ahead!'

And he explained to his penpal, firmly and clearly over two sides of neat writing, exactly what he wanted him to do.


The coach from Sticklebury pulled into Westburn bus station exactly on time, circled the central cafeteria, and drew in at the furthest bay.

Laura and Oliver leaned as far as they dared over the safety railings, craning to see the passengers as they stepped down.

'There he is!' Laura pointed. 'In the red jacket.'

Oliver stared.

'He said he was taller than average,' he complained. 'He didn't say he was on stilts!'

'He's not all *that* tall,' Laura argued.

But Oliver, who was an inch shorter than Laura, remained unconvinced.

As Simon fought his way out of the clump of passengers milling around at the rear of the coach Laura and Oliver could see that tucked under his arm was a large cardboard folder, tied with string.

'He's brought the stuff all right, then,' remarked Oliver, somewhat appeased.

'I knew he wouldn't let us down,' said Laura.

She leaned across the railings, and yelled:

'Over here, Simon! We're over here!'

He heard, and spun round. Quickly he spotted her in the crush of people waiting behind the railings, and waved. Then he dived into the nearest underground walkway, and joined them less than a minute later.

Simon and Oliver greeted one another with some reserve. It was quite clear to Laura that Oliver was still a little bit peeved about the difference in their heights; and Simon had not yet forgiven Oliver for the tone of his letters. But the two of them struggled valiantly to be civil, and, with Laura walking between them, they started off towards Green Lane, Oliver pointing out Neighbourhood Watch Signs along the way as if they were greater spotted cuckoos.

'There's certainly enough of them about,' Simon admitted after a few streets. 'You must have had an awful lot of robberies. I can see why you were so desperate to get my expert help.'

Behind Simon's back, Oliver made a quick face which Laura took to be a sarcastic, if silent, reference to Simon's fast growing self-esteem.

'The plan worked out all right, then?' she asked.

'Worked out?' Proudly, Simon tapped the large cardboard folder under his arm. He was striding along so fast that Laura and Oliver had to scurry to keep up with him. 'The plan worked *beautifully*. It couldn't have turned out better.'

'Oh, yes?'

Maybe Simon was still feeling sensitive about Oliver Boot. Maybe Oliver's tone was a little too sceptical. But Simon stopped in his tracks. His face set, and he laid the large cardboard folder down on the low brick wall beside them.

Oliver and Laura drew closer.

With his blunted fingertips, Simon struggled with the knot in the string. After a moment's hesitation Laura came to his aid with her unbitten nails. She tugged the string away, lifted the folder and tipped it gently.

Across the top of the wall slid a fan of glossy, black and white photographs.

Laura and Oliver turned them over, one by one, slowly. They were absolutely perfect. He'd followed his instructions to the letter, and made three copies of each photograph. And he'd done them beautifully.

He stood behind them, watching their reaction. He wasn't fidgeting at all, Laura noticed. Not even tapping his feet, or squirming or twitching.

'These photos are just marvellous,' breathed Oliver. He didn't even try to hide the admiration in his voice. 'You *couldn't* have done them better.'

He tipped all the prints in the folder over, and started once more at the beginning.

The first photograph was taken from Simon's bedroom window. It was a picture of the end of the alley, and showed both the rickety porch where the man in the faded green corduroy jacket lived, and part of the cathedral wall behind.

'You've even managed to fit in a bit of fancy stained-glass window!'

'That is our famous window of Saint Cecil of Sticklebury,' Simon declared with unabashed civic pride. 'People come from all over to look at that.' As Laura and Oliver exchanged a brief glance, he added wistfully: 'Unfortunately, I've only managed to fit in a sliver of Saint Cecil's left heel.'

'It's more than enough!' Oliver assured him. 'To *check*, I mean. There can be no doubt it's Sticklebury Cathedral, so it's clear which house this is, too.'

Oliver had warmed up considerably towards Simon since seeing the photographs. His tone, Laura realised, was positively friendly now.

'Zoom lens,' said Simon as he turned over to the next print.

This one was taken from Simon's own doorstep. It showed the porch again, but so much closer that it was possible to make out the ancient, rusting iron plate above the doorway.

## The Hermitage

'Clear as could be!' admired Laura.

'Nothing special,' said Simon. 'A bit of care with the focus and exposure, that's all.'

The next print showed the man in the green corduroy jacket stepping out of his porch, and looking appreciatively up at the sunshine.

'It took me hours to get that one,' said Simon.

'He looks so *nice*,' Laura said wistfully. 'And he was very kind to me. I can't believe he's a real, deep-dyed villain.'

'But anyone else would,' said Simon, 'if they were shown the rest of these.'

He turned to the next print.

This one was taken from the steps of the porch. Not only was the little cardboard sign above the letter box visible, but the print was distinct and easy to read.

'Close-up lens,' Simon observed casually. 'And flash, of course.'

In order to take the next photograph, he had stepped back into the street. Now only the left side of the porch could be seen because he had swept the viewfinder across to take in both the creeper and the neglected window.

'I rather like this one,' Simon couldn't help remarking. 'I think it's a finely balanced composition in its own right. I particularly like the way the light shimmers on the filth of the glass panes. I think I might enter this one for some competition.'

Behind his back, Laura and Oliver exchanged another brief look.

Simon turned the photograph over.

'These next few weren't easy,' he told them. 'Not easy at all. For one thing I had to be sure I had plenty of time to take them. So I had to keep following our man all round Sticklebury, trying to work out his plans for the day.'

'Weren't you supposed to be in school?' asked Laura.

Simon flushed.

'I go most days now,' he insisted. 'But not always. And on this particular afternoon it was lucky I didn't, because he happened to drift off to the cinema. I saw him safely inside our local Odeon, then rushed back and took these.'

He spread them along the top of the wall.

'Close-up lens again. On a tripod because of the exposure time, of course. I couldn't use a flash because of the reflection from the glass panes.'

Laura and Oliver weren't really listening, but they nodded admiringly as they examined the photographs. Six clear shots of the inside of the room, two taking in what was quite obviously the same blistered window sill as before, four concentrating more on the room's contents. The photographs had been taken with such care and precision that even the labels on the cartons stacked along the wall could be read clearly. The spots of ink splashed over the front of the filing cabinet had not yet been wiped off, Laura noticed. The office baskets on the table were beautifully in focus. And the old cake tin full of pens was only a tiny little bit blurred.

'And now,' boasted Simon. 'The most impressive photograph of all.'

He started to explain the technical difficulties he had encountered with this particular shot, but neither Oliver nor Laura paid any attention. They were both staring at the photograph again. It was Lady Melody's letter, as clear as print, clipped to the rainbow-coloured notepaper, and tossed in the basket.

'That *is* the letter you particularly wanted, isn't it?' asked Simon.

He was unnerved by their joint silence.

'Oh, yes,' breathed Laura. 'That's the one.'

Oliver turned to face Simon squarely.

'It's an enormous relief, seeing these photos of yours,' he confessed. 'Right till the very last moment I worried that you might turn up here with just a pile of blurry, indecipherable smudges.'

Simon bridled.

'I don't see why!' he snapped. 'I *told* Laura I could

do pretty complicated things with my camera.'

'Yes,' Oliver pointed out. 'And you told me in your letter that you tell terrible lies, as well.'

'But not about photography!' Simon protested, outraged. 'I'd never tell lies about something as important as that!'

Oliver said loftily into the air around him:

'It beats me how liars expect other people to know which subjects they still consider sacred. . . .'

All the blood drained from Simon's cheeks. He looked as though he had been slapped. He was clearly only moments from tears.

Laura's soft heart couldn't bear it. She said sharply to Oliver:

'It was silly to waste time worrying about Simon's photographs, because Simon has given up lying for *ever*.'

She turned to Simon.

'Haven't you?'

And Simon answered firmly and clearly, to spite Oliver:

'Yes. Yes, I have.'

The opportunity seemed rather too good to miss.

'And fidgeting and squirming and twitching.'

'Yes.'

'And missing school.'

Simon Huggett took his time over this one. But Laura kept her eyes firmly on him, and, like a rabbit helplessly transfixed by a snake, he was finally forced to reply:

'Yes. If you like.'

In for a penny, in for a pound, thought Laura.

'And biting your nails'.

Simon spread his fingers. They did look horrible,

all chewed and red. And it had been humiliating to need help untying the knot in the string.

'All right. I'll try.'

'*And* not treading on the yellow swirly bits of the carpet.'

But, faced with this endless catalogue of his failings, Simon Huggett was turning a little bit sullen.

'Steady on, Laura,' muttered Oliver, in warning.

So, graciously, Laura conceded the yellow swirly bits of the carpet. She'd done Simon Huggett's psychologist enough of a favour already, she reckoned. She'd pulled his socks up for him a good three quarters of the way.

'All right,' she agreed amiably enough. 'Keep the carpets.'

The silence that followed was a little bit awkward. It was Oliver who broke it by distracting them both. He reached out and pointed to two squares of thin card clipped tightly together at the back of Simon's folder.

'What's in here? Another photograph?'

Hastily Simon pushed it under the folder, out of sight.

'Oh, that. It's not in the series. It simply happened to be on the same film.'

But Oliver was curious about the sort of photographs Simon took when he wasn't working under orders.

'Can I have a look?'

Simon appeared dubious.

'It's nothing much. Just something I took from my bedroom window one rainy day.'

'Oh, go on. Let us look.'

Clearly, Simon was torn between pride in his work and simple embarrassment. Oliver took advantage of his mixed feelings, and slid the photograph out from between the two squares of card.

He laid it on the wall on top of the others, and gazed at it in astonishment.

'Why, it's Laura! How extraordinary! Laura standing in the pouring rain, grinning all over her face. What a wonderful photo!'

Simon was pleased.

'Do you really like it?'

'Like it? It's *amazing*.'

Delighted with this response, Simon dared turn to Laura.

'Do you like it, too?'

Laura considered. Generally she didn't much care for the photographs people took of her. Though she nodded and smiled politely when she was shown them, she usually found something she didn't like at all in the expression on her face, or the way she was standing, or what the wind had done to her hair or her clothes. But, she had to admit, this photograph of Simon's was both strange and striking, and little things like her sodden hair and her drenched clothing didn't seem to spoil it at all. She looked so happy standing there – almost ecstatic – under a cloudburst without a care in the world. It suddenly brought back to her in full force that glorious moment of freedom and release.

'That was the best moment of my entire life,' she told the two of them. 'The moment I realised Miranda didn't exist. That is *exactly* how I felt. You caught it *exactly*.'

'That's photography,' Simon said proudly.

'That's why I love it. There I was, sitting staring out of the window, bored stiff, and then I saw you there, looking so extraordinary, as if something perfectly wonderful had happened to you. Radiant, as if you had seen a Christmas angel, or something. And I simply had to take a photograph. I took my camera off the bed, and set it up behind the flapping curtains. Then I called "Pssst!", and held the curtains back. And you turned your head.'

'So that was why you were trying to attract my attention.'

Simon blushed.

'Yes, for the photograph. And it's a present.'

Now it was Laura's turn to blush. And as the other two leaned over the wall, picking one copy of each particular shot from the pile, and sliding them inside the large brown envelope that held Lady Melody's last, threatening letter, she took another good long look at the photograph in her hand.

She trailed behind Oliver and Simon as they made for the pillar box on the next corner, and pushed the large brown envelope inside it. She was still glancing furtively at the photograph.

Really, the longer she looked at it, the more she liked it.

The burglar must have written back almost at once, but still it seemed the longest wait. Laura felt little short of grateful when, hanging about at the bottom of the stairs for the fourth morning in a row, she finally saw the familiar rainbow-coloured envelope slip through the letter box and float to the floor.

It had been a nerve-wracking vigil. Wait and see, Oliver had told her, equably going about his other concerns. But Oliver was made of sterner stuff. Laura was unable to keep herself from fretting, day after day, night after night, in case the thief did not write back. What would they do if, after a whole week or so, there was still silence? Would Oliver insist on reporting the whole affair to the police?

The very idea filled Laura with the deepest unease. Each time she thought about the burglar now, she couldn't help seeing in her mind's eye one of Simon's superb photographs – the one where the man was stepping out of his house and smiling as he looked up at the sunshine. If they told on him now, he'd go to prison. How could a man like that stand it? A man who smiled up at the sun that way would go mad locked up day and night away from the streets and the wind and the weather.

And all for a few video machines and computers and electric carving knives! She couldn't bear to think about it.

But whenever she did, she knew one thing: she couldn't be the one to tell on him. She knew she wouldn't be able to stand it afterwards. She wouldn't breathe freely any more, knowing he was stuck in a prison cell, and just for trying to help other people. It would be a living misery for her as well as for him – like all those dreary, guilty weeks when she felt so awful about Miranda – as if she herself were somehow imprisoned too.

Oh, please, *please*, for both their sakes, let him show sense!

Her heart thumping, Laura tore at the envelope
and ran her eyes down the sheet of notepaper

> The Hermitage
> 2A Cathedral Close
> Sticklebury

Dear Lady Melody,
   Your letter gave me quite a nasty turn, I
must say. And I didn't at all like the names
that you called me – liar and cheat and thief.
Look at it my way. I only ever stole things
like electric hedge shears and food processors
and microwave ovens, that people can
manage without perfectly well. The people I
tried to help are cold and hungry and
homeless. It's very easy for someone of your
sort to get on a high horse and act
sanctimonious about what I've done. But I
don't expect you to begin to understand –
you who were brought up with your ponies
and Chinese porcelain dolls and tigers' heads
on the wall! What would someone like you
know about it?

He sounded so dismissive of people 'of her sort'
that in spite of the fact that she wasn't Lady Melody
at all and so none of the things he wrote really
applied to her – well, not much, anyway – Laura
found herself flushing.

But you've been smart enough to find me
out. And I'm not so daft as to think I'd be any
use to anyone mouldering away in a prison.
So you win, Lady Melody Estelle Priscilla
Hermione Irwin. That's the end of all my
little burglaries. You have my word on that.

So he had said it! *You win, Lady Melody*! Relief
flooded through her.

106

But don't think for a moment you've put me off. I'm simply going to find some other way to do what I do – some way that can't be interfered with by some well-to-do little girl who never lacked for anything much herself going all self-righteous on me.

And I'm glad you won't miss your letters from Miranda. I can't say I'd be very pleased to hear from you again, either!

Your former penpal

Though the handwriting was level and clear, the signature was nothing but a billowing whorl, like the squiggle on top of an expensive chocolate.

Pale-faced, Laura stuffed the letter deep in her schoolbag, out of sight, and ran as fast as she could to the corner.

Oliver's reaction to the letter was rather different.

*So you win, Lady Melody*, he read aloud. *You have my word on that.* 'What is the word of a liar worth, Laura?'

Laura was silent. She hadn't thought of that. How horribly complicated these things were!

'Surely we have to trust him,' she said at last, spreading her hands. 'What else can we do?'

'Nothing,' said Oliver. 'So we have to trust him. But he's not sorry, you know. Not in the slightest.'

'No,' Laura said. 'And if he does stop stealing it won't be because he's suddenly realised what he's doing is wrong. He'll stop just so he won't end up in prison.'

They walked on. Oliver kept his eyes down as

he thought, while Laura ran her gloved fingers along the film of frost on the wall.

In the end Oliver said a little doubtfully: 'But he is stopping, after all.'

'That's what we wanted,' Laura said.

But somehow as they walked on together, making ghosts with their breath in the chill morning air, both felt that there was something thoroughly unsatisfactory about the whole business. Admittedly, thought Laura, it was a relief – a very great relief – that the letter was not actually brimful of savage threats of revenge.

And she couldn't pretend she'd expected repentance and gratitude.

But she hadn't expected this either. No. Nothing like this curt and hurtful note agreeing to her terms in such an unwilling and ungracious fashion, and even hinting that because of Lady Melody's sanctimonious interference the homeless and cold and hungry would go without a bit of help that would mean far, far more to them than Lady Melody's purity of mind could ever mean to her.

The letter left a nasty taste.

And it was not the sort of uncomfortable feeling that faded, either. She knew from the sinking in the pit of her stomach that the longer she thought about it, the worse she'd feel.

No doubt about it. He was the thief – but she felt guilty!

As they turned into the last street, she couldn't help confiding in Oliver.

He listened in amazement.

'Guilty? You feel guilty? *You?*'

'I can't help it,' Laura said. She pulled nervously

at her gloves' cold clammy fingertips. 'I feel terrible, Oliver. I feel as if I've sailed in and stopped this man from stealing any more electric carving knives, but at the same time, without meaning to, I've stopped him helping people with no food to carve!'

Oliver knitted his brows. His spectacles began the long, slow slide towards the frosty pavement, stopping only just in time as his face cleared.

'Right, then!' he said. 'You'll just have to help these people yourself.'

'Myself?'

'Why not?'

Laura considered. No reason on earth why not.

'And would you help?'

'If you like.'

'Oh, Oliver!'

She felt so happy and relieved she couldn't help throwing her arms around him and hugging him till his glasses shot off right there outside the playground gates where everyone could see. Another brilliant Oliver Boot solution! It was a bother, and it would take time. But others did it, so why shouldn't they? And, yes, it would stop her feeling so horribly, horribly guilty.

As Oliver bent to retrieve his glasses, he found himself almost crushed in a desperate stampede. It seemed that almost everyone in the class had spotted their arrival and was running towards them, shrieking.

'Have you heard the news?'

'Nobody has to write any more letters!'

'The penpal scheme is finished!'

'It's all off. Mrs Coverley has just had a note

from a man who says he's from the Sticklebury Water Board.'

Laura drew in her breath sharply. So she was not the only one to get a letter this morning. He must have been busy!

'What did the note say?' Oliver was asking.

Jessica pulled a face, and shrugged.

'Mrs Coverley won't tell us. She says the details are not fit for our ears. But it seems that there's something really funny in the Sticklebury water, and all our penpals must have drunk too much because not one of them will be writing any more letters for a while.'

Nikhil's eyes shone.

'Not one of them,' he breathed ecstatically. 'Not *one*.'

But Jessica was desperate to tell Laura and Oliver the rest of the story.

'And Mrs Coverley doesn't believe a word of it! She says if anything as serious as that were true, it would be on the news. And the letter isn't even written on proper Water Board paper. So she thinks the Sticklebury children must have got together and planned a rude and lazy way of getting out of being our penpals.'

'And she's *disgusted*.'

'She said so several times.'

And after the class had settled in their seats that morning, Mrs Coverley said so several times more. 'So *rude*!' she muttered, raising her arms to pat her bun firmly back into place. 'I can scarcely believe it. This is the very last time we ever get involved with penpals. From now on, we shall do something else entirely.'

Oliver was never one to miss an opportunity. As soon as he heard this, he took to nudging Laura hard in the ribs.

'Quick!' he urged. 'Go on! Now! Remember what we were talking about in the playground? Well, this is your big chance to get everyone helping.'

Laura's eyes widened at the thought. Get everyone helping? The whole class? Mrs Coverley too? Was Oliver expecting her to speak up in front of everybody without becoming all hot and tongue-tied?

Well, he was absolutely right, as usual. Without giving herself a moment in which to get nervous, Laura lifted her hand.

'Mrs Coverley?'

'Yes, dear?'

'If we're going to do something else,' said Laura, 'I have a really good idea what it could be.'

Mrs Coverley listened in amazement as Laura Irwin stood up behind her desk and spoke her mind. Where was the sensitive plant she'd put beside Oliver Boot only two terms ago? Quite gone. And in her place this confident, outspoken – yes – *fearless* child was making quite an impassioned little speech about the cold and the hungry and homeless.

And Mrs Coverley was so intrigued, she even failed to notice when her hairpins began to slip. Before Laura had finished detailing her plans, gravity and the weight of the bun won the battle, and all Mrs Coverley's pepper-and-salt hair cascaded freely round her astonished face.

*

Laura sat with her head propped on her elbows and stared, absorbed, out of the classroom window. Above her, the glittering Christmas decorations spun lazily. Outside, the snow kept falling as it had fallen all day, and, as she watched, the so-familiar view of street and kerbs, of pavements and high stone walls, was silently giving way to a strange world of glistening white.

Around her, the din was considerable. It had been all day, as one group of children after another jostled round the five desks pushed together and piled high with goodies collected from everyone and everywhere imaginable. What had become known throughout the whole school as Laura's Great Christmas Sale for the Cold and the Hungry and Homeless had been a wonderful success. Even the parents and the teachers had come. Everyone had at least a little money to spend. Everyone had at least one or two small presents to buy. And everyone found at least something they fancied.

From his seat behind the stall, where he had been all day, Oliver proudly announced his current running total.

'A hundred and sixty-three pounds!'

Mrs Coverley murmured her growing amazement, and almost everyone else in the classroom made some remark or another each time the total climbed a pound or two. Only Laura paid little attention. She was still watching her snowflakes exert their quite extraordinary magic, laying their shimmering blanket over the dull grey playground she knew so well, transforming the stunted trees and miserable bushes into outlandish and astonishing shapes. She didn't care how much they made any more. Leave that to Oliver. She'd sit here, content with a job well done, and watch the world change in the cold, blue dusk-light.

'Laura?'

It was Oliver. He had left his post for a moment. He stood in front of the desk, a torn piece of newspaper in his hand.

'Laura? Are you all right?'

'I was just watching the snow fall.'

Oliver glanced out of the window. So far as he could tell, the snow was falling no differently than usual, and so there seemed to him to be little to watch.

'Look what I found.'

He held out the shred of newspaper.

'What is it?'

'Read it and see. Someone must have used it to wrap a toy for the stall. I found it lying on the floor just now.'

Laura took it. One side was nothing but a torn half of a photograph of marathon runners. On the other was the first few lines of an article.

### Strange Find

Last night, police expressed themselves 'still mystified' over the curious discovery in Westburn Town Hall Lavatories of a huge stack of undamaged electrical goods, including videos and televisions and microwave ovens.

P. C. Anna Fairway told our reporter: 'Some of these things were stolen weeks ago. People are coming from all over town to claim things.'

The lavatory attendant, Mr Ben Phillips, said: 'I only dropped off to sleep for a moment. I can't think how—

The rest of the article had been ripped away.

Laura looked up, but Oliver had already darted back to his place on the stall.

Laura lifted the desk lid. They ought to send a copy of this to Simon. He'd be delighted. Only a couple of days before, he'd sent them a cutting from his own Sticklebury paper. Now Laura drew it out and read it again.

### Baffling Benefactor Bewailed

Local charity shops are bewailing the disappearance of their most generous benefactor, the mysterious masked man who used to turn up twice a week or more bearing everything from electric hedge clippers to stereo speakers.

'We're really sorry he's stopped coming,' said Mrs Joanna Solomon, (54). 'But I like to think he's still helping us – maybe in some other way.'

Mr William Warren, (27), agreed. 'He cared so much about what we were doing. I can't believe he's given up helping completely.'

But both agree – very sadly – their baffling benefactor has not been seen for some time.

The snowflakes kept tumbling from the sky as Laura sat wondering. What would the thief do now? What had he said in his letter? *I'm simply going to find some other way to do what I do.* Would this, too, turn out to be something dishonest? Did people ever change their habits so easily? Could they?

Well, Simon Huggett had, that was for sure. He'd changed a lot. As if to be assured that changes in people were really, truly possible, Laura opened the desk a second time and pulled out the letter Simon had sent along with the cutting.

Flattening it on the table, she read it again.

Dear Laura and Oliver,

Do you know, at first nobody noticed anything different about me when I got home after my weekend with you in Westburn – except my mum said I looked taller, which is ridiculous since I was only away from home two whole days.

But then I got to stay up till eleven one night because nobody realised I was still in the room. When my dad finally turned round and noticed me, he was astonished. Why Haven't You Been Fidgeting and Squirming and Twitching As Usual, he asked. He sounded quite put out and sent me off to bed at once, but Mum looked really pleased, and had a whisky.

I haven't been able to keep much of an eye on our friend, I'm afraid, because I went to school every single day this week! I even played football. In my boots! And I managed to undo a knot in the laces without using my teeth because my fingernails have started growing. Now Mum says I've changed so much since the weekend with you that there must be something really funny in the Westburn water.

Dad says it was his idea of buying me a really good camera that's made me so much easier to live with. He's going to fix a cupboard up as a tiny developing room for me for Christmas.

How are you both? I hope you are quite well.

    Love,
    Simon

Yes. No doubt about it. Change was possible. Simon Huggett was living proof of that. But would the burglar bother? She wished she knew. It seemed so strange to interfere in someone else's life this way, and yet never find out exactly what happened.

She sighed.

Oliver's voice rang out over the hubbub.

'A hundred and seventy-six pounds!'

A hundred and seventy-six pounds. It was a good deal of money. It probably made up for quite a few electric carving knives and hedge clippers and things. And what would the burglar think of them if he knew how much money they had raised? He'd probably be astonished. He probably believed that Lady Melody Estelle Priscilla Hermione Irwin was far too busy rocking her Chinese porcelain dolls to sleep in their ivory cradle, or dusting the tigers' heads on the wall, to find time to organise a Great Christmas Sale.

She'd let him know, then! She would write and tell him! He'd said he wouldn't be very pleased to hear from her again, but she wasn't going to let him get away with believing that she was just sanctimonious and interfering, and no use at all! She had clean envelopes left over from grisly writing-to-your-penpal days. And the inside of her desk was littered with Christmas cards, some hardly crumpled at all, and one or two even written in pencil. Arif's, for one. And his was lovely. Arif wouldn't mind if she very carefully and gently rubbed out his name and wrote her own – or rather, Lady Melody's.

'One hundred and eighty-six pounds, forty pence!'

Oh, splendid! Keep it coming, Oliver!

The softly falling snow entirely forgotten, Laura buried herself in her note to the burglar. When she came to telling him about the amount of money

116

they'd raised, she left a space. She could fill that gap at the very last moment, when she would write in Oliver's final, magnificent Great Sale Total, just as the bell rang at the end of the day.

A week later, on the last afternoon of term, Oliver walked home with Laura through the chilly blue dusk. The two of them were laden with every last forgotten item from the shared double desk and the presents that they had bought in their own sale. Trailing behind Oliver on the end of some string was a monstrous yellow plastic duck on wheels, at least twice the size of his baby sister.

'I'll just have to keep it at your house till Christmas,' he warned Laura. 'It's far too big to hide at our house.'

'It's just far too big,' Laura warned back. 'She'll probably break her neck falling off it.'

'She'll love it,' said Oliver. 'Being fearless.'

Laura's own spoils were more modest: a couple of boxes of soaps for her aunts; a book on bread-making for Mrs Bandaraina next door; and a delicate wooden frame for her parents.

'What are you putting in that frame?'

'Simon's photograph of me. The one he took in the alley. It's a surprise.'

'They'll love it,' said Oliver. 'It's a smashing photo.'

Laura scooped Mr Whiskers up from where he was sleeping on the garden wall, and started introducing him to Oliver's duck.

Oliver interrupted.

'You've got another letter, Laura!'

Laura spun round with Mr Whiskers in her arms. Oliver was right. Once again, sticking from the letter box, there was the corner of a rainbow-coloured envelope.

This time Oliver seemed to know at once what was expected of him. He strode across and prised the envelope out of the letter box, then tore it open and read aloud:

> The Hermitage
> Sticklebury

> My dearest Lady Melody,
> Each time I step outside freely into the alley and look up at the sunshine, I feel so grateful to you. I almost believe that if I'd been found out by anyone else in the world except you, I would already be locked away. What I was doing was dangerous and foolish, and I'm so glad you forced me to stop before I got into the most terrible trouble.
> Tremendous news about your Christmas Sale! Keep up the good work! With all my previous experience sorting out some of the things I took that weren't working properly, I myself am just starting up in business – an electrical goods repair shop – profits to charity!

Oliver lowered the notepaper and stared at Laura.

'Good,' Laura said firmly. 'I *knew* he'd think of something.'

A smile of pride and pleasure lit her face.

'How does the letter end?' she asked, after a moment.

Oliver read out:

> So now we're absolutely straight. Take care. Happy Christmas.

'I *told* you he was a really nice man.'

'You did,' said Oliver. 'You were right all along.'

Laura looked anxious.

'But we're not absolutely straight yet. Not absolutely. Not while he still thinks that I'm Lady Melody....'

'You think you ought to tell him?'

'I don't know.' Laura's look of anxiety turned to doubt. 'I mean, it's all worked out so well, hasn't it? Why risk changing things now?'

Oliver bit his lip.

'He does seem to have become quite fond of you – as Lady Melody, I mean.'

'You think he'd be a bit upset if he knew?'

'He might be disappointed.'

'He might be hurt.'

They stood eyeing one another dubiously. Then Oliver said:

'Truth isn't the only virtue, is it? There's always charity as well.'

Laura stared. Was it possible that strict old Oliver Boot was mellowing just a little at last?

'After all,' Oliver went on. 'You've done so well so far, doing it your way. You don't want to risk spoiling things just on some tiny little principle....'

Laura still stared at him in sheer astonishment. Where was the Oliver Boot she knew?

'So,' Oliver finished up tranquilly. 'I think I should just leave it, if I were you.'

Laura's look of astonishment softened into a little private smile which she buried deep in Mr Whiskers' fur. In his own way, she couldn't help thinking quietly to herself, Oliver Boot was really becoming quite human.

119

'Right, then,' she said. 'I think I'll just leave it.'

Fishing her key out from around her neck, she turned and led the way to the back door.

And the huge yellow duck on wheels trundled noisily behind them all the way round the house.

# READ MORE IN PUFFIN

For children of all ages, Puffin represents quality and variety – the very best in publishing today around the world.

For complete information about books available from Puffin – and Penguin    and how to order them, contact us at the appropriate address below. Please note that for copyright reasons the selection of books varies from country to country.

**On the worldwide web**: www.puffin.co.uk

**In the United Kingdom**: Please write to *Dept. EP, Penguin Books Ltd, Bath Road, Harmondsworth, West Drayton, Middlesex UB7 ODA*

**In the United States**: Please write to *Consumer Sales, Penguin USA, P.O. Box 999, Dept. 17109, Bergenfield, New Jersey 07621-0120.* VISA and MasterCard holders call 1-800-253-6476 to order Penguin titles

**In Canada**: Please write to *Penguin Books Canada Ltd, 10 Alcorn Avenue, Suite 300, Toronto, Ontario M4V 3B2*

**In Australia**: Please write to *Penguin Books Australia Ltd, P.O. Box 257, Ringwood, Victoria 3134*

**In New Zealand**: Please write to *Penguin Books (NZ) Ltd, Private Bag 102902, North Shore Mail Centre, Auckland 10*

**In India**: Please write to *Penguin Books India Pvt Ltd, 706 Eros Apartments, 56 Nehru Place, New Delhi 110 019*

**In the Netherlands**: Please write to *Penguin Books Netherlands bv, Postbus 3507, NL-1001 AH Amsterdam*

**In Germany**: Please write to *Penguin Books Deutschland GmbH, Metzlerstrasse 26, 60594 Frankfurt am Main*

**In Spain**: Please write to *Penguin Books S. A., Bravo Murillo 19, 1° B, 28015 Madrid*

**In Italy**: Please write to *Penguin Italia s.r.l., Via Felice Casati 20, I–20124 Milano*

**In France**: Please write to *Penguin France S. A., 17 rue Lejeune, F–31000 Toulouse*

**In Japan**: Please write to *Penguin Books Japan, Ishikiribashi Building, 2–5–4, Suido, Bunkyo-ku, Tokyo 112*

**In South Africa**: Please write to *Longman Penguin Southern Africa (Pty) Ltd, Private Bag X08, Bertsham 2013*